The Demon Accords

Volume One

Stories from the Demon Accords Universe

By John Conroe

This book is a work of fiction. All of the characters, organizations, and events portrayed in this novel either products of the author's imagination or are used fictitiously.

The Demon Accords:
God Touched
Demon Driven
Brutal Asset
Black Frost
Duel Nature
Fallen Stars
Executable
Forced Ascent
College Arcane
God Hammer
Rogues
Snake Eyes
Winterfall
Summer Reign
The Accords Compendium, Volume 1

Cover art by Gareth Otton.

Author's Foreword

After many requests for follow-on stories regarding many favorite side characters, I started the Demon Accords Compendium. Partway through the writing process, I decided to break it into two volumes. This is primarily to get the stories out faster at novella length rather then wait until the collection reached critical mass for novel length. If you're happy with this development, thank my wife. She pointed out that the stories could be released in groups as I completed them, rather than make fans wait a full six months, like most of my books seem to take. Volume 2 will follow very quickly, and then the next full book in the series, Demon Divine.

The first story in this collection is a look at the beginning from Lydia's point of view. As you might imagine, she has her own take on things. Story two steps back further in time and is told from a spot just over Alex Gordon's (Gramps) shoulder. The last two are more contemporary and follow the events of Summer Reign. *Volume 2 will have more contemporary stories to set the stage for the next in the series. I hope you enjoy reading these as much as I enjoyed writing them. Also, at the end, please take a moment to sample a new series I've started, Zone War, the first book of which is due out late summer 2018.*

Thank you so much for caring about my characters as much as I do. Oh, by the way, this will be my last year balancing both a financial career and a writing career. As of January, 2019, I'll be a full-time writer, with my leg chained to my desk. About time, right?

John Conroe
Spring 2018

First Impressions

It all started for Chris with a trip to a NYC club. But what was that like for the others? Let's take a look through Lydia's eyes and find out...

"Five minutes," Stevens said from the driver's seat of the limo.

"Thanks darling," I said with a smirk. Stevens was an unabashed player, a skirt chaser... or a philanderer, as my mother might have said. But only with humans, and never with staff. For some reason, he got ultra-embarrassed when it was brought up in front of Tanya. I could literally feel the heat rise in his face from my spot in the backseat.

Tanya's face stayed blank... until Stevens' attention reverted to the road ahead. Then she gave me a little smile. Nothing wrong with her sense of humor.

Her smile changed and she turned it fully on me. I sighed. "Of course we will dance," I said. Her smile broadened. I couldn't read her mind like Nika could, but I had been reading my girl her whole life. She could convey entire volumes with very, very small shifts of expression or body language, at least if you knew her well enough.

She smoothed her short white dress against her thighs, a sign of happy anticipation. She *does* love to dance. Not as much as fighting or winning at business, but a close third. I glanced across her to the stunning blonde in the red dress on her other side. Nika, the third of our fearsome three. Red, white, and... black. My dress was the black one.

Nika's eyes were unfocused and I suspected she was *checking* things out at Plasma before we got there. She frowned, still unseeing.

"Everything copacetic?" I asked.

"Vadim seems concerned," she said, still concentrating.

I sat up a little while Tanya chose to slump back in her seat. Prior history had shown that a concerned head of security often meant a cancellation of the night's dancing.

"And?" I asked, slightly annoyed that I had to drag it out of her.

She frowned again, then her eyes cleared and she turned to look at me. "Some NYPD, off duty. One's a regular, the other two are new, likely rookies. One of those has piqued his interest," she said.

"Cops? Is he sure?"

"Yeah, the senior guy is a Plasma regular; you'd know him if you saw him. Vadim always lets him through the line. Looks like he's leading a celebration of sorts."

"So what's the deal with the one rookie?"

"Well... he's got violet eyes," she said, frowning again.

"That's it?" I asked, making no attempt to hold back a snort. "What's the matter with violet? Is Vadim smitten or something?"

Galina, who sat across from the three of us, put her hand over her cell phone and turned her sharp eyes on me. Oops. Might have gotten a little loud there. But for good reason. Tanya had perked up as soon as I had spoken. I'd take heat from the Ice

Queen anytime if it resulted in my girl being even remotely happy.

Point made, Mama Fang went back to her business call. I looked at Nika and raised both eyebrows. *Well?* I thought as loud as I could.

"Well, the eyes caught Vadim's attention, and on top of it, he thinks the guy is a fighter," Nika said, giving me a slightly apologetic smile.

"He's a cop. They're supposed to be fighters—it comes with the job," I said.

"Yes, but he's different. Got a different feel to him," she said.

"And?" I pushed. It honestly wasn't usually this hard with Nika, but mind reading isn't an exact art and she's the best there is, so I had to be patient. Or at least as patient as *I* could be. While I waited, my hands grabbed a laptop and I signed into the security system at the club.

"Not sure. I can't explain it. But he's not like any human I've ever scanned. Nothing overt or seemingly dangerous, but, well... curious," she said.

The camera by the front door was very high quality, but the detail of the three men in front of Vadim wasn't good enough to deflect my sudden concerns. One of the men, the shortest, stood in a confident stance. Not enough information either way.

Tanya was looking at her hands on her legs, but now her eyes cut my way. I sighed again. "Dancing is still on, but I think it'll be you and Nika. I'm gonna have to at least put some eyes on this cop," I said.

She held my gaze and when I didn't blink, she gave me a little nod. She'd be happier if all three of us were dancing but she understood how seriously I took her safety.

The limo braked smoothly, Stevens handling the big car as well as most Darkkin could. We were at the back of the club and a small army of Darkkin streamed out of the darkness to surround the car and cover our exit from it.

"Clear," was the soft word from the young Darkkin security guard who was leading this effort. Trenton was his name, I seemed to recall. The three of us *moved*—clearing the car and into the building in a literal blink of an eye. Galina chose to follow at normal speed, still talking on her ever-present phone. She was young to hold the responsibility that she did, but much of that was due to her daughter. Still, she was at least three times my age and for all that, she'd taken to modern technology like a wino takes to booze.

Inside, I could feel the beat of the band, even as far from the dance floor as we were. Nika and Tanya headed toward the staff rooms while I veered off and found the club manager.

"Three cops, newly arrived—I'll take their table," I said. She raised both eyebrows. "At least for the first round," I said. Brows still raised, she just nodded. "Second floor, east alcove bar," she said as I pulled on a Plasma t-shirt over my LBD. The shirt was a small but it was still loose enough to cover the top of the dress and make it look like I was regular staff. Grabbing a tray, I headed out into the club.

The joint was packed, pretty much as it had been ever since we'd opened it. The place was in the black, profit wise, in less than six months after the ribbon cutting. The whole idea of the club came from Tanya, silently conveyed to her mother on paper.

Humans are weird. I know I used to be one, but it's been long enough that I find it harder and harder to relate to them. Some were dressed in black Victorian clothing, fashions that I actually remembered. Others wore regular club clothes, but more and more, the clientele was shifting to the goth look. I spotted my cops right away, sitting at a small table near the railing. Nika was right—the senior cop was a regular, and enough of a skirt hound in his own right to give even Stevens a run for his money. He looked slightly annoyed, most likely because none of the staff had approached their table yet. He spotted me beelining for them and relaxed ever so slightly.

I swished up to them, slipping into the role. "Ah, hi. I'm—" the player started but I interrupted before he could finish. "You're Officer Henderson. Welcome to Plasma. I am Lydia," I said, putting on my *vampire* voice, whatever the hell that was. Honestly, I'd been skeptical about the whole vampire club thing but Tanya had been adamant it would both be a huge hit and that the world would not take it seriously. She'd been so right.

Henderson was tall and good-looking in that confident alpha way a lot of cops had. The guys with him were young, early twenties, both staring at me, eyes slightly widened. The one to his left was boy-next-door bland, excited to be out but trying to act cool. Tall and thin. The other one... had honest-to-God purple eyes.

Other humans likely wouldn't really notice them in the low light of the club, but to my eyes they popped. A fantastic violet color that I had never seen on any person in my life. He was shorter than the others, maybe five-ten or five-eleven, but much better built. Wide shoulders, and his thin sweater clung to a nice chest, while the pushed-up sleeves revealed muscular forearms attached to large, strong-looking hands. Even features, good cheekbones; he was cute, but different. His smile was quick, too brief, and his purple eyes had something about them—a sadness maybe.

Henderson ordered a Moscow Mule, while tall and skinny asked for a Bacardi and Coke. Purple eyes quietly requested a Corona—with lime.

I turned and headed to the closest bar, which was just across the room. It was a single bartender station and not meant for waitress orders, but I wanted to keep eyes on the eyes, so to speak. The vampire behind the bar turned to warn me off his station, then realized who I was. His mouth shut, thank God, and he moved out of my way while I prepared the drinks.

Watching without being obvious is literally an inborn Darkkin talent, so I had no trouble observing my cops even as the two youngest basically stared my way. Tanya had written out the underlying psychology of her business plan, and she had hit the thing right on the head. On some level, humans sensed the presence of predators when we were among them, but their modern ignorance of things supernatural blunted their instincts. The result they felt at Plasma was what Nika described as a delicious spike of adrenaline with no obvious source. Nothing bad ever happened to humans in Plasma—we were ultra careful about that—so the instinctive thrill of our presence kept them titillated but comfortably unaware.

I had read reviews that compared Plasma to a haunted theme house mixed with an exclusive nightclub venue. Humans found it fascinating to observe us but rationalized to themselves that we were just actors following a script. We were just being ourselves, which was hugely appealing to Darkkin normally forced to conceal our nature, hence the plentiful employees willing to work as servers and wait staff, jobs usually beneath our pride.

The two young cops were staring at me, their instincts likely screaming at them to keep eyes on the predator. Henderson was already making conversation with a nearby table of gothedup office workers, leaving the two newbie cops to talk about the club. I shamelessly listened in from across the room.

"Dude, this place is *off the chain*!" the tall, skinny one said.

"It's actually pretty cool," purple eyes said. He had the tiniest of accents.

"They must spend a fortune in contact lenses, don't you think, Chris? Did you see our waitress's eyes?"

"Yeah, they all have really cool makeup, but look how the staff moves. I think they hire dancers or acrobats or something," Chris Purple Eyes replied.

I brought them their drinks, freely putting my Darkkin grace on display. It *was* kind of liberating to move as we normally did. Henderson took his drink with a nod, attention focused on the blonde he was chatting up at the table behind them. Lanky was trying for cool but his eyes widened a bit and I heard his heart speed up. Purple eyes narrowed his peepers at me, just slightly, and his heart rate stayed surprisingly even. "Thank you," he said, his partner just staring. I withdrew to the shadows and watched.

They were both kids but young Officer Eyes was different. Calm, focused, polite, and... sad. Oh, this one would be major bait for the real goth girls in the club. In fact, he was drawing a few stares of his own, but for all his alertness, he didn't seem to notice. Instead, he studied everything else around him, dismissing his fellow humans but focusing his attention on the bartender, frowning slightly. His partner gulped down his rum and Coke, a not uncommon side-effect of the subconscious fear humans felt at Plasma—our bar sales were through the roof. Officer Eyes sipped his beer like it was the last one he'd ever drink.

When I noticed Officer Henderson tipping his copper mug to drain the last dregs and that the Bacardi cop had already finished his, I brought a second round to the table.

"Compliments of management. Thank you for your community service, Officers," I said, showing off just a little as I smoothly snatched up the empties and laid out the fresh drinks. Eyes was still holding his first beer, and it was only a third gone. His eyes locked on mine as I served them. I made sure to lean close when I put his new beer in front of him, taking a slow, deliberate sniff. "You boys must be fresh from the Academy to smell so healthy and in shape," I said, letting my eyes linger on their throats here and there.

"Six months out of it, ma'am," the rum drinker said, his new beverage already half gone. "We just came off probation," he said, holding out his glass for his interesting young partner to clink with his bottle.

I had thought to check out these cops, clear my concerns, and get back to my *real* work. But this kid was so oddly different that I couldn't, in good conscience, stop observing just yet. Too self-possessed, too calm and controlled, too intriguing looking and too damned delicious smelling.

No Darkkin ever imbibed from a human visitor to Plasma. That was rule one and only older, strongly self-disciplined vampires were allowed at the club. This was the first time I regretted that rule.

With my odd cops under immediate control, I cycled back to check on T. She was holding court in the staff lounge. Not that she was doing anything as deliberate or calculated as *holding* court but, nonetheless, that was the de facto result.

Darkkin are drawn to Tanya like moths to light. I've seen it time and again. They don't even have to see her; they can literally feel her presence, I think. What I found in the lounge was Tanya sipping blood from a mug, listening as vampires spoke to her. She nodded, shrugged or shook her head when needed, which wasn't all that often. The fact that she didn't speak, hadn't spoken in fifteen years, didn't seem to dampen her admirers' enthusiasm. She listened to them all with patience beyond her years. There was only one kind of admirer who would be turned away—the ones who couldn't contain their physical attraction for her. Male or female, she would quickly and succinctly decline their advances. She wasn't interested. If they pushed, she'd push back. I was certain she wasn't asexual; no one who dances like she does could be, but she hadn't found anyone who piqued her interest in that way.

I had heard the rumors; hell, I'd had some of the same thoughts myself. That her traumatic past had blocked her emotional development, stunted her feelings. I didn't believe any of them any more. It was more like she was... waiting.

One of the regular wait staff came in. "Oh, Lydia. Your table needs another round. Well, at least two of them do," she said to me.

Nika raised an eyebrow at me, smirking.

Yeah, he's interesting as hell, but I don't know why—I thought at her. Her smirk quirked into a real smile and she nodded in agreement before turning to keep an eye on T and her current petitioner.

Blue, blue eyes glanced at me then away, telling me that Tanya was, on some level, aware of my back and forth with Nika, and a bit curious.

I circled back to the boys out of blue, bringing another Mule and another rum and Coke. Officer Eyes was only just starting his second Corona. He watched me as soon as I entered their space, eyes curious, alert, and nowhere near as intoxicated as his friends were getting.

The pattern repeated itself several times, waitress duty, Tanya duty. I judged T as being just a short time from abandoning her faithful admirers and dragging Nika to the dance floor. Taking another swing by the coppers, I took a new approach. Coming up behind the intriguing one, using every bit of Darkkin skill and stealth, I leaned down by that sweet-smelling neck.

"Falling behind your friends a bit there, ay North boy?" I said in his ear. He didn't jump but I finally got the heartbeat flutter I'd been missing. He paused a second, taking in the tiniest gulp of air, then turned his head to meet my gaze.

"How do you know I'm from the North and not Canada?" he asked, puzzled. *I'm* next to his throat and *that's* what he focuses on?

I didn't let on how gratifying it was that my ear for dialects hadn't let me down. "Your accent. Kinda like a Canadian, but still not exactly like it. Ay, ya hoser," I said. "So you look like you could use a shot to catch up with your pals."

His response was instant. "No, one of us needs to keep his wits about him in this wicked nest of vampires," he said with a smile. It came across as joking but he meant it.

"Oh, you'll be safe enough, Officer. We don't eat our civil servants," I said.

Mission accomplished, I spun around and headed back. On impulse, I glanced back, catching him watching my exit. A drunk guest took a swipe at my behind, but humans will never catch a vampire who doesn't want to be caught. That second Corona was almost gone and I decided to grab him another. For some reason, I wanted to see his guard go down. Below, I heard soft

Darkkin voices warning that Tanya and Nika were headed out for the next song. Instead of joining them, I decided to see what Officer Eyes thought of my girl. Fresh beer on tray, I circled the floor, coming back to my table. Officer Eyes was gone. I did a quick scan. No, he was by the railing, looking down. The house lights dimmed as they always do when our dancing is about to begin. Because it's such a regular occurrence, many of the club guests knew what that meant.

"Tatiana, Tatiana, Tatiana, Tatiana," began to echo through all three levels of the club. It was now too dark for humans to see much, but I could see Officer Chris like it was merely dim. He seemed to be systematically searching the crowd below. The excitement in the place was palpable, the chanters shortening their call to just "Tat."

Below, on the dance floor, the band began a new song, one of Tanya's favorites. People at the railings began to shove a bit, jockeying for a better vantage point. My subject had stopped his search and turned his oh-so-interesting gaze on the dance floor. The song exploded and the spotlights blasted the center of the floor. I didn't have to look to know that Tanya and Nika would be killing it. Hell, normally I'd be right there with them. It was too loud to hear heartbeats, but I could see the pulse jump on my officer's neck as he took in the sight below him, finally reacting to something in a normal way. Suddenly, he stepped back, shocked for a second, and I just knew he'd seen my girl. She has that effect on almost everyone, mesmerizing the masses without effort. But his stunned look changed to something else, something that greatly disturbed me—recognition. Now *my* guard came up. How could he recognize her?

And then he did the unthinkable: He *looked away* from *her* and went back to his scan of the bar area below. There was something almost frantic about it and it held back my first impulse, which had been to grab him and drag him away for questioning. He had recognized Tanya, but he was looking for someone else, and he was most anxious to find them. His head scanned the crowd then suddenly snapped back, his eyes narrowing, expression changing from worried to another look that I knew intimately—predatory.

Now he was moving, heading for the stairway down. He jigged and jived his way through the crowd. I shifted to keep him in sight, and his head snapped my way. Bright violet eyes locked onto me for a split second, then he dismissed me, his head whipping around to look back. He tensed up for a moment, then relaxed minutely as he spotted whoever had dragged his attention away from Tanya. He leaned against a post, indexing his body toward the dance floor, but his face was angled toward the bar. I *moved,* sliding over to look down where he was looking. Nothing and no one stood out, at least to me, but he was locked like a hound on a scent.

The song ended and the regular house lights came up. Officer Chris headed down the stairs, moving through the crowd, his body language telling me he was on the hunt. For who?

"They're leaving the floor," the club manager said in a low voice, the Darkkin equivalent of a PA announcement. I still couldn't see who the cop was following, no matter how hard I tried. There was a sense of someone moving through the crowd, but I couldn't quite get a view of him. Chris the cop seemed to have no trouble and now his path took him behind a couple of the Darkkin bodyguards assigned to keep anyone from getting into the employee-only section.

I watched him walk right behind one of the guards, just slipped right through two experienced vampires.

"Hey, there you are. What do you think?" Nika said suddenly. I turned around and found her standing by my side—alone.

"Where's T?" I asked, looking behind and around her.

"She went through the door," she said, pointing. "She wanted..." Her voice trailed off and her eyes narrowed as she picked up something on her Nika radar. "Attack! Tanya's been attacked!" she said, voice loud by vampire standards.

I *moved*, breezing past the two guards. "This way," I said. I felt Nika and the guards behind me as I followed Tanya's scent trail, along with the scent of the cop and something else—something that stunk of sulfur.

Vadim was suddenly by my side and when I hit the next door hard enough to tear it from its hinges, I followed it and let him by me to deal with anything or anyone hostile. My only thought was Tanya.

There she was—standing in a pool of blood, hers by the scent, her white dress now scarlet and torn. Yet she stood tall and strong, unbroken skin, healthy and whole, showing through the sections of torn and ruined cloth. She was holding up the cop, who leaned like a drunk against stacked supplies. A silver blade and two silver spikes lay on the floor in front of them.

Vadim cocked his arm, ready to kill the first human ever in Plasma and instead locked up tight at the brain-freezing sound of "Nyet!" that came from... Tanya.

I felt her command seize up my body even as my brain processed the fact that she had just spoken a word, had yelled out a command. The whole group who had responded turned to look at our natural-born princess. Then Nika and I were moving, shoving through the others to get to our Tanya.

Details speared my mind. She was holding him. He was reeling from blood loss. Her blood was spread everywhere but she was fine—perfect. A smear on the corner of her lips. She had drunk his blood—a lot of his blood. And now she protected him. And had spoken for the first time in fifteen years.

Behind me, I sensed Galina arriving. "What is all this?" she asked in Russian.

"Mother, I was attacked. This man helped me. The attacker ran down the hall and out the back exit," Tanya said, also in Russian, not smoothly but clearly understandable.

Guards turned and *moved* after the attacker. Nika was right up on Chris the cop, studying him. "The attacker was thin and reedy lo-" Tanya started, still speaking Russian, but Nika interrupted her.

"He's lost a lot of blood. He needs fluids, like now!" our blonde mind reader said in English.

Tanya turned to me. "Lydia?" she asked. From her, it was a cry for help. Not again, never again. Not another death laid upon her fangs on my watch!

"I'm on it," I said, *moving* like I'd never moved before. We were in the storage section, so I only had to travel back through the torn doorway and grab the first fluids stacked on the pallets in the hallway. Behind me, I heard Galina ask the cop his name.

"Chris... Chris Gordon," I heard in that lightly accented voice.

"He's a cop," I said, popping back into the room, handing him the drink. He took it, looked at it, eyebrows raising in astonishment, then, despite reeling from blood loss, surrounded by hyped-up vampires, he laughed. He was staring at the drink, red Gatorade, and it took a second for the irony to hit me. I found myself preoccupied by the look on Tanya's face as she watched his every move. It was a... possessive look. Oh my.

"He's here with some cop friends. I watched him follow some guy who was following Tanya," I said.

Despite being wobbly, he got the cap off the bottle and took a healthy swig. Funny, but his heart sounded pretty good. Tanya must have either not taken as much blood as she'd lost or... No... that couldn't be... Could it?

Nika was also studying Officer Chris, and I was dying to know what she *heard.* Her eyes widened. "He is a hunter of something... demons, I think. At least *he* thinks he is. He thinks maybe we will kill him now and he will fight us, but is almost relieved. Almost as if he would welcome it," she said, all in Russian.

Chris frowned, clearly not understanding but somehow thoroughly annoyed with us.

"Well, you people don't need me for your private conversations, so I'll just be going," he said.

He stood, weak like a kitten but ready to go. One of the guards, Arkady, stepped forward aggressively, face transforming into full-on vampire. "You go nowhere, human blood bag," he snarled. No, no you idiot! I thought. Arkady was old, didn't he see the signs? Nika glanced at me, eyes wide.

A mix of emotions flashed across the young police officer's face. Fear, followed by anguish, followed quickly by rage. Nika gasped. I ignored her, too concerned with the next few seconds. Chris leaned down and grabbed one of the bloody spikes on the floor. He wiped it on his sleeve and then took a knife fighter's stance. Shit, shit, shit! The situation was devolving quickly.

"Fuck off, Fang! Why don't you come over here? I'll show you where I keep the good silver," the young idiot said to the pissed-off warrior vampire.

Before anyone else could screw up, before I could even form a thought, Tanya *moved.* So fast even my vampiric vision couldn't follow her actions. She just simply was there—standing between Arkady and the cop, her back to the deadly silver spike, every bit of her focused on the threatening vampire. And she was growling. A deep, deadly growl that somehow conveyed instant death to the much larger vampire. It was a crystal clear message that if he twitched, she would end him.

For his part, Arkady was smart enough to realize that he stood no chance if she wanted him true dead. In fact, no one in the building other than Vadim stood a chance against her, and even then I'd put my money on Tanya. Vadim was her instructor and sparring partner, but I don't think my girl had been going all out in their almost daily contests. I don't think she'd been that motivated. But that had changed. In the last five minutes, a great deal had changed.

"Enough!" Galina said into the tension. "Arkady, get the clean-up gear and get rid of this blood. Tanya, calm down. No one will hurt him." Her voice stayed even but her orders to Arkady were as firm as her assurances to Tanya were real. One of her gifts. She recognized that something major had just happened with her daughter, but I wondered if she realized just what. Observant but not always sensitive, our Galina.

Arkady *moved* backward and down the hall, wisely clearing himself from the immediate danger zone.

Tanya relaxed and turned to check over her cop. And he was *her* cop. I could see that possessiveness in every inch of her being. Whoa, whoa, whoa!

Nika's eyes kept flaring and I was dying to know what the kid was thinking that kept surprising her so.

"My apologies, Officer Gordon. Arkady is a trifle overzealous. But where are my manners? I am Galina Demidova; you have met my daughter Tatiana. This is Nika. You have already met Lydia. This is Vadim, our head of security," Galina said, pointing us all out.

Recognition of the name Demidova flashed across his face. Then he turned and looked at Tanya, then back at Galina, visibly comparing the two. They looked enough alike to make him realize the truth of her words. The truth that had set the Darkkin world on fire twenty-three years ago. The truth that almost started a civil war. Nika smirked at the kid and he turned his puzzled gaze on her. Realization flooded his features.

"Some can," Nika said to something he was thinking. I could easily guess the trail of his thought. Damn, this kid was fast. Low blood drunk and surrounded by vampires and he was arriving at answers faster than any normal human should.

"So is your daughter Tatiana or Tanya? I'm confused... more confused?" he asked. Of all the things to ask, he chose to ask about the girl. Either super smart or super lucky.

"Tatiana is her formal name, Tanya is her short name. Like Jennifer and Jen," Galina answered.
"Officer Gordon, would you be so kind as to tell us what happened here?"

He looked back at her for a second, then glanced over all the vampires, looked at Nika, met my gaze, and finally looked directly at Tanya. Then he nodded, as if it was a big decision.

And launched into a story. A story of visions, demons, Hell, and our princess. He reached out and grabbed an inventory clipboard, flipping the paper over, his bloody fingers smearing the white with red. A short, stubby pencil appeared from his back pocket and he started to draw. The truly odd part was that he never once looked at what he was drawing, instead continuing to talk about demons from Hell in our club. He was done so fast, I thought he must have just scribbled, but then he handed the picture to Tanya and slumped back on his crate. I looked over her shoulder, feeling Nika and Galina moving up beside me to look as well. It was sharp, detailed, and sophisticated, showing a clear depiction of a man with a knife, body angled to attack a spiked and wounded Tanya.

"That's your guy... er... demon. Demon ridden, if you want to get technical. I call them Hellbourne. The body is just a shell," he said.

"How do you know all this? How *can* you know all this?" I asked, mouth running away from brain.

Galina gave me a glare. I don't really answer to her although I have to keep on her good side if I want my job to run smoothly. North boy thought about my question, brow furrowing.

"The clergy say that I'm God Touched. Personally, I think He bitch slapped me. We have agreed to disagree on that point," he said.

"Clergy?" Galina asked.

"Yeah, well, the various churches come to me for their tougher exorcisms. The prayers and holy water routine doesn't always work," he said with a casual shrug.

"And *you* do?" Galina pressed.

"I don't use their techniques. I'm more of a hands-on kinda guy," he said, shrugging again. "The entities that make up most possessions are pretty easy to yank out and send back to Hell. Plus I'm nondenominational."

I knew from the moment I saw him that the kid was different, but this? This was too much. He looked around at us, swigging his drink. Wiping his mouth with the back of his hand, he continued. "You all seem to be having a lot more trouble believing me than I'm having believing all this," he said, waving one hand at us and especially at Tanya. Girl was focused on him like a spotlight.

Galina, who had frozen into contemplation at his words, suddenly shook herself out of the spell. "I'm afraid we need to ask you for your clothes, as we must burn all of Tatiana's blood that has been spilled. Nika, please get Tatiana cleaned up. Lydia, would you find Officer Gordon some new clothes?"

Nika dragged Tanya toward the staff rooms while I surveyed the kid, guessing sizes, which, by the way, I'm pretty damned good at. Vadim grabbed a garbage bag and stepped up to the kid, so I shot up the hall and followed the ladies into the staff lounge. The shower was already running in the dressing room and I heard *her* voice again. "But is he really okay, Nika? Is he going to be... alright?"

"You heard his heart, T. It evened right out as soon as he started to drink the alligator stuff Lydia gave him," Nika answered.

"It's Gatorade, Nika," Tanya said with a little relieved laugh. I listened shamelessly as I rummaged through lockers and boxes of uniforms. I could listen to her voice all night. Fifteen years and now she was back. Which reminded me. I took out my phone and texted *She spoke!* then went back to my rummaging. Shirt was easy; we had boxes of them. Pants, though, that took a few moments till I found the last pair of leather pants we had on hand. The kid had a waist as narrow as most Darkkin males.

I judged he would fit our most common size. The shower cut off and I shot back out into the hallway.

The kid was leaning against the stack of crates the drink almost gone, wearing just a pair of black boxer-briefs, which in my opinion was the best answer you could have to the age-old question of "briefs or boxers."

"Damn, Northern! Do you live at the gym or what?" I asked, handing him the clothes. I knew my words would be heard up the hallway, inside the dressing room, and I started a countdown in my head. Ten, nine, eight...

The kid wrestled the pants onto his well-built bod in a most enjoyable manner, barely getting them on when I heard the staff lounge door open behind me. His eyes snapped up at the sound, his body freezing, still holding the shirt. A quick glance back showed Tanya gliding down the hall, herself obviously rushed into some of her spare clothes. She was drinking him in and when I looked at the kid, he looked like Vadim had punched him in the face. Hah!

Tanya went right up to him, ignoring everyone else in the room, her focus now on the odd pendant that hung between his sharply defined pectorals. Looked like an arrowhead and a feather. She glanced at his eyes, then back down, and I read a sudden shyness in her actions. Very subtle, but there if you knew what to look for. She reached out to touch the soft feather, then looked back up at him. He nodded permission and she took the whole amulet into her hand. I saw her mouth open to ask a question but before she could, he reached up and pulled the leather thong over his head and then over hers. Her eyes widened and her mouth snapped shut.

"Aww, is cute that we are giving friendship gifts now," Arkady suddenly said from behind me. Really, dude? Have you completely missed what's going on? Did you forget the part where she was ready to kill you?

"Well, seeing as the Hellbourne walked within two feet of your blind ass on his way to kill Tatiana, maybe you don't have a friggin' clue what you're talking about," Chris said. Damn, he's cheeky too. The points kept adding up.

"You call me Tanya. Not Tatiana," our princess suddenly said, staring him in the eyes.

He didn't know what that meant and I could see the self-doubt form in his eyes. "Oh, er, sorry. No offense," he said. Oh shit, he was the anti-player. Not totally a bad thing, but *some* game would be good.

"She wants you to call her by the name her friends and family use, not her formal name," I said. A tiny light of understanding bloomed on his face. He nodded. Then he got weird. He looked her up and down, only his eyes were unfocused. Then he backed up, using one hand to steady himself while he continued to stare at her in that strange zombie way.

"Explain please," Galina asked, waving a hand at the necklace.

"Well, when I banish demons, I give off a lot of... power. Objects made of stone tend to absorb some of that power and sort of store it, like a battery. I usually carry a piece of carved soapstone with me when I exorcise a house or apartment, Indian fetishes. I leave it behind as a protection. If any other demons come around, they will shy away from the stone. They've helped a few people who, for one reason or another, tend to draw demonkind."

"Is that arrowhead such a fetish?" Galina asked.

"Better. I've had it since I was a kid and it's absorbed some power every time I have kicked Hellbourne ass. Which would be something like, oh about... thirty-seven times or so. Not counting exorcisms."

"Why?" Tanya suddenly asked.

"Er, what?" he asked.

"Why do you give it to me?" she asked.

"Well, the demon that wants your blood will be back. If it is during the day tomorrow, I'll probably be able to nail his ass. But this should protect you if I'm not here. It will make you invisible to him and it will repel him, as well. But I want to boost it if I can. I'll feel better if it is ramped up a bit more," he said. He paused and looked uncertain.

Galina leaned forward. "So do it!" she ordered in her typical way.

Annoyance flashed across his face and I half expected him to tell her to shove it. Nika smothered a snort, earning herself a quick glare from Galina.

"Well, I'm gonna spill a drop of my own blood and I'm just wondering..."

"Go ahead. We can *probably* control ourselves," Galina said, eyes narrowed. Actually, my impression was that we had better damned well control ourselves or Tanya would object—strenuously.

I've seen hardened combat vets and old career cops shake with fear when presented with the reality of vampires, but this kid was cool as a cucumber. Just plucked a pocket knife from his personal stuff, flicked it open, and aimed it at his right index finger. He paused for a moment, visibly concentrating, and I suddenly felt the hair on my neck lift just slightly. Something was happening. Then the knife darted down and the tip kissed the end of his finger. He squeezed the pad of his index finger between his thumb and middle finger, a big red dot blossoming.

Every vampire in the room smelled that blood and we all leaned forward, if ever so slightly. Tanya's eyes flared and she tensed, turning slightly to let us all see her expression. The young cop standing so close to her missed all that, his attention on the arrowhead, which he turned over and pressed the blood onto.

"Ah, that needs to be against your skin, um, like under your shirt," he said, suddenly choosing to be nervous. A room full of vampires, a bleeding finger, and he gets nervous talking about naked skin.

Tanya gently, slowly pulled the arrowhead from his hand, pulled the front of her shirt open and carefully placed the amulet between her breasts. *Now* the kid's heartbeat chose to race like an engine.

He took a little step back, wiping his finger on his pant leg. After an awkward second, he let his eyes unfocus and tilted his head to look her over.

"I don't know what you people do during the daytime, whether you go to sleep or lie in coffins or whatever, but you two," he said, pointing at Nika and me, "might want to hang close to her. It can probably protect all three of you. You can leave Arkady out by the door as bait." He was confident again, folding the knife and tucking into a pants pocket.

Arkady hissed at him but the big bodyguard was spraying bleach solution on the walls and floor, destroying Tanya's invaluable blood. Without even a flinch, Chris focused on putting his shirt on. They ran a tad small, on purpose, and my selection was spot on. It was a fun show and Tanya was so focused on watching it that she didn't notice the rest of us paying just as much attention to him. When he was done, it looked like he'd spray-painted it on. Damn I'm good.

"Officer Gordon, you are remarkably blasé about this situation. Most of your kind are scared witless by our presence, if in fact they live through the introduction. How is it that you aren't?" Galina asked.

The friggin' kid snorted. "You mean the vampire part? Most humans haven't been hunting Hellbourne since they were twelve, either. Actually, I don't think any other humans do what I do. Compared to demons, you all aren't that scary. Plus I'm too damned tired at this point to give a crap."

I knew nothing of demons, except that something had slid past all our security like it wasn't there and almost killed one of the deadliest vampires on the planet. And this kid had been hunting them since puberty if not before. And his comment about being tired? Did he mean tired tonight with low blood, or tired of life?

Everyone had gone quiet, mainly to process his words. That would be unnerving to any human. This kid thought we were offended. His hands came up in a *calm down* gesture. "Oh, you're scary enough, all right. Top predators and all. I'm sure that Lydia there could twist my head right off before I got done blinking, but really, what's the worst you can do? Kill me? Torture me, then kill me? Big whup! Hellbourne can trap or foul my soul, haul me to Hell," he said. Tanya's eyes darted my way, narrowed when he mentioned me ripping his head off. Shit, what are you trying to do, kid? Get me in trouble?

"You really aren't afraid of dying, are you?" Nika asked.

"You tell me, mighty Kreskin. Hell, I've outlived my death by about fifteen years," he said, "Actually, I've been on borrowed time since the moment of birth, twenty-three years ago. Well, twenty-three in seven more days. If I get there."

Vadim spoke just as I realized what that meant. "Halloween? You were born on Halloween?" he asked. That was Tanya's birthday.

"Yeah. Spooky, isn't it?" he asked with a sardonic smile. He had no idea. I glanced at Nika, then Galina. Both of them looked blank, which in Darkkin body language was the same as shock.

"Do you know the time of your birth?" Galina finally asked.

He frowned, looking around at us, baffled by her response. "Well, I'm told it was midnight. But I don't really remember, being pretty young and all," he said. Oh my God. The kid was a wiseass. I knew I liked him.

"Killing is not the worst," Arkady, of all people, suddenly said. "We could Turn you."

Chris turned to him, expression incredulous. "How is that worse? Let's see, if the legends are true, I would be stronger, faster, tougher, and live a lot longer. The downside would be what, exactly? Liquid diet?"

My own face must have mirrored the kid's by this time and I glanced aside at Nika. She kept her eyes on him, but her head shook gently side to side. He wasn't lying. He wasn't afraid of what we might do.

"Soul is lost when Turned," Arkady said, his voice actually dramatic, like his was the final word on the matter.

If anything, Chris's disbelief deepened. "My soul... lost? Why would my soul be lost? Yours aren't!"

Oh my. My phone buzzed in my pocket. I ignored it, waiting to see what would come next. Nika spoke suddenly into the silence. "He believes we all still have souls," she said, frowning.

From the moment I awakened as a vampire, I had been told that I had a new life, a life that could possibly last forever. But if I died a second time, it would be a true death. And there would be no afterlife for us.

"Yeah, because you do. I can see them," Chris said. Then he turned and began to stuff his wallet, cash and personal stuff into his leather pants pockets.

"You can *see* souls?" Tanya asked him. He turned and looked at her. He nodded. "Yes. Yours all look white to me. Humans usually are some shade of blue."

My phone buzzed again, insistent. It would only get more so, but this was too intense to even think of checking it.

Galina stepped forward a pace. "Let me get this right: you think you can see souls, and you think you can see *ours?*" she asked.

"Yup. I see all kinds of shit, some of which you apparently don't. How else can I see Hellbourne? They can only occupy and use bodies that are soul-free. Meat shells," he said.

My phone buzzed again. No, way. Too busy. "What does white mean?" I asked him.

He shrugged like it was no big deal that he'd just told the Darkkin race that their myth story was a lie. That salvation wasn't denied them.

"I don't know. Probably that you are a different species or something. You're each slightly different. Tanya's is wicked bright." He leaned back and drank the last bit of his Gatorade. He already looked quite a bit better.

"White means evil!" Tanya suddenly said. She had been frozen, watching him, but now she looked disturbed.

"What?" he asked, frowning. "Since when does white mean evil? Why would you think that? Black means evil. Oily, greasy, stomach-turning black," he said, shuddering as he remembered something. "I don't think you're necessarily evil, any more than wolves, bears, or tigers are evil. I'm not going to lie, though. You're all pretty damn eerie, though."

Tanya's expression changed, changing from upset to angry. Angry he wasn't listening to her words, angry he wasn't taking this seriously. "You lie! You are a liar! You know we are evil!" she all but yelled. Not good.

My damned phone buzzed in my pocket again. My own fault... you can't send *that* message to *that* individual and expect to be ignored. But this was too real-time important and that would be my rationale for taking too long to respond.

Chris was dumbstruck. His face went through a host of emotions: hurt, disbelief, anger, and did I mention hurt. He'd, purportedly, fought a demon, been fed on by a vampire (thus discovering that we were real), almost to the point of death, faced down a dozen of said vampires, and revealed that he was apparently, a demon hunter, almost from birth. But Tanya freaking out about her own identity issues (because when you accidentally kill your nursemaid as a child, you get the mother lode of issues) was the thing that rocked his world. Or maybe it was her calling him a liar.

The anger won out. "Righhht," he said, his expression closing down. He set the empty bottle down and turned to Galina. "Well, thanks for the clothes and Gatorade and shit. Unless you're gonna eat me, I'm leaving." He stood up and marched forward. Two things struck me; one, he really wasn't afraid of Vadim, and two, he was much, much steadier than he had been just minutes ago.

Both of theses mental items fought for my attention as the young cop walked out of the hallway, through the broken door, and out into the club, leaving the rest of us standing in various states of bemusement. Tanya immediately turned to me, her face screwed up with self-doubt. I read her concerns before she could voice them. Nodding, I followed the kid out into the club, his scent easy to track, even among the sweaty, hormone-ridden masses. A waiter passed me. "The cops you were watching left with some female guests," he said. The thing about Darkkin is that we hear *everything*. Most of the staff knew about the attack and much of what was going down.

The only remaining cop, and the only one that mattered, was standing at the table he'd had with his friends. A new group had taken it over and one girl asked if he worked at the club. "Oh hell no! Just wearing the colors," he said, tone cold enough to make the girl flinch. A little brutal, and yes he was still angry, but it was decidedly for the best if she lost interest immediately, if my guesses were true.

He turned around, putting his jacket on. "Your friends left with the girls they were hitting on," I told him, stopping him in his tracks.

"Lucky them. Did they pay the tab?" he asked. "No," the bartender thirty feet away said, only loud enough for me to hear. "Hundred and ten dollars."

I shook my head at Chris.

"Bastards! How much?" he asked, jamming a hand into his pocket.

"One ten. But it's on the house," I told him.

He frowned, shook his head, and pulled out a money clip. Peeling off three fifties, he pushed them at me. I took them, a sudden flash of insight telling me that rejecting his payment would further alienate him.

He walked out of the club, not knowing I was following. *Nika, I need a car and driver, asap,* I thought. Outside, I found him pacing while he waited in the cab line. A black Aston Martin pulled around the corner and parked, the driver, Trenton, keeping his eyes on me. The kid finally got a cab and climbed in.

I slid into the Aston Martin, nodding at the cab I'd seen our young cop get into. Trenton pulled smoothly up behind it and I finally pulled out my phone. There were six texts, all the same: *Update now.*

Time was up. I typed furiously, as fast as my Darkkin speed would allow me.

Tanya attacked at Plasma. Rookie police officer intervened. She was gravely wounded and drank from him. She spoke when we arrived on the scene. Cop is some kind of exorcist. He says attacker is a, "Demon from Hell in a human shell." The demon walked past Darkkin security without detection. Cop can sense and see them. Tanya <u>*exceedingly*</u> *concerned with safety of this cop. I am following him to be sure he gets home.*

And press send.

The response came in seconds. *How badly was Tanya injured? How much blood taken from human? What authorities know? Analysis.*

I sighed. The first parts were easy. It was her final command that would be... taxing.

T lost substantial volume. Wounded by silver in both shoulders. Ingested several pints from cop. No authorities know. Analysis: Cop has some arcane abilities. He says given by God. Tanya is <u>fully healed</u> with just one feeding. Should be on her way to Dr. S now. Cop should be showing more signs of blood loss. Isn't. T extraordinarily focused and protective of cop. Press send.

Then after a second, I added a line—the most impactful. *I believe she has Chosen.* Press send.

I watched the phone, but nothing happened. Up ahead, the taxi carrying young Chris was threading smoothly through traffic and Trenton was staying back far enough to make it difficult for anyone in the cab to even see the black Aston.

My phone buzzed. *G called. Similar report. Lighter on details. Then <u>spoke</u> to T, herself. Incredible. Continue your present course. Make sure this officer gets home safe. Nika has very interesting details. Confirm cop healthy.*

Damn it. I was dying to know what Nika had picked up, but here I was trapped in the car babysitting a cop.

"He's stopping," Trenton said. I glanced up in time to see our subject get out of his cab next to an apartment building.

"Drive past and let me out. Circle back and wait for me," I said, watching the young cop enter his building.

Trenton let me out half a block ahead and I ghosted into the shadows, moving back toward the building.

One wall was in darkness and I climbed it, Clinging to the side, sticking to every shadow and bit of gloom I could. I could hear nothing from the elevator, but moving around the outside a bit, I picked up the plod of tired feet climbing stairs. A door opened and closed on the second floor and footsteps walked down a hallway. A key turned in a lock and another door opened. Then a fridge door. Pouring sounds, followed by a cracking sound which took me a second to identify as an egg. Followed soon by two more eggs. Chugging sounds. A sigh. Glass on countertop. Feet plodding. Shoes falling to floor, one at a time. Sound of a body hitting a mattress. Steady breathing. Strong breathing. I strained my hearing to its utmost. Heartbeats. I focused, eliminating the old ones, young ones, small ones until I found just the right one: strong and even. Sleep tight, Officer Eyes.

Back on the ground, I located the car and moved quietly through the darkness till I could slip inside.

"Where is Tanya?"

"Vadim says she is at the mansion. Dr. Singh is giving her a check-up," Trenton reported.

"Okay, let's go."

When we got to the massive brownstone that Galina was using as her current home in the Big Apple (she tends to change them up often), I found Doc Singh wrapping up his thorough check-up of our princess. She had her clothes back on and was recounting for a bemused Singh, his assistant, Nika, and Galina, the play-by-play of her encounter with the demon and the cop.

"You say you didn't see this *man* till he had already shot you?" Singh asked in disbelief.

"I heard the door and turned but it was like there was this fuzzy blur, then I felt a hit in my left side, then my right and it burned, Doctor Singh, like a hot coal. Then Chris came in and drove the guy off."

"Yes, my dear, silver burns a great deal, which is why I'm trying to wrap my head around your condition," he said.

"Which is?" I interjected.

"Perfect."

"Completely back to normal?" I asked, a hint of disbelief finding its way into my own voice.

"No... better. Her already superior vitals are slightly elevated," the doctor said, shaking his head. "Just who is this cop? I want a sample of his blood."

"NO," Tanya said, her eyes narrowed. Instant response, instant anger. And she didn't blink as she glared at the doctor who had taken care of her all her life. More evidence for my case.

"Ah, I was just interested in its composition, Tanya. You heal very fast, but silver slows all of us down," he said, holding both hands open, clearly shocked at this new Tanya.

For her part, Tanya's expression changed from an angry frown to a worried frown. "I took so much, Doctor. He can't give any more," she said, turning to me. She might be talking now but I could still read her body language.

"He's fine. He went home, drank fluids with eggs, and went right to sleep. Heartbeat strong and normal," I said.

"You saw his home?" she asked, eyes opening at the thought. The good doctor exchanged glances with Nika, who smiled, and Galina, who frowned.

"He lives in an apartment which I didn't see, but the building looked pretty good," I said.

"Does he have a roommate?" she asked. Oh, I see where this is going.

"No one in the place but him," I said.

"Oh, I thought there might be someone... else," she said.

"He strikes me as the loner type. He was very ill at ease in Plasma," I said.

"He doesn't like vampires," she said, making it a statement.

"I don't think it's that, kiddo. His accent is from upstate, way, way upstate. He completely ignored most all of the people in the club except for me and the bartender and, of course, you when you were dancing," I said.

"He saw me dance?" she asked, suddenly shy like a middle schooler. She's almost twenty-three, the deadliest fighter I know, with killer business instincts, but in some ways she is still a child.

"I'll say. Knocked him for a loop, but then he started looking for the Hell thingy, almost frantic to find it. Remember, he said he had a vision about you?"

She blurred across the room. Damn, that girl can move. She was back on the exam table, holding a certain piece of paper with a familiar picture on it.

Doc Singh had apparently not seen it and she handed it right over. Then a new frown appeared. "He shouldn't have done that," she said.

"Done what, dear heart?" Galina asked.

"When he pulled out the second dart, a piece broke off inside my chest. I pounced on him and drank from him and he... he reached in and pulled out the piece," she said, pointing at a table in the corner where I could see a silver knife and dart and a small piece of silver. "I was preying upon him and he helped me. Why would he do that?" she asked.

"He likes you," Nika said. "And to answer your earlier question, he has no girl in his life, or even close friends."

Tanya didn't say anything but instead just looked down at her lap, her hands smoothing her sweats on her legs.

"So what's the story with him?" I asked Nika. Everybody in the room turned to look at our family telepath.

"Christian Gordon, rookie cop. As you say, he grew up way, way up state. Something tragic happened to his family many years ago. It involved one of those demons. He's the only survivor. He had a few flashbacks, especially when Arkady got in his face. He was telling the truth. He's been hunting demons his whole life and basically exorcises them by willpower or something. Something supernatural. It's incredibly dangerous, as we saw by Tanya's near call," she said.

"Why was he so nonchalant about us?" Galina asked.

"He doesn't expect to live very long. He's also sad, tired, and lonely, and has been dealing with Hell since he was a child. He understood our advantages but he was already invested in

Tanya's survival. He thought we would kill him. I think he almost welcomed it," she said. I snuck a peak at Tanya. Blue eyes as big as quarters soaked up every detail of the story with utter and complete fascination. She blinked at the last part and turned those eyes on the rest of us.

"We won't. Kill him," Tanya said. It wasn't a question, more like a statement of fact. Or maybe... maybe a command. Her first ever. Actually, her second.

"Did you tell Senka all that?" I asked Nika, pointedly not looking at Galina and ignoring Tanya's words . I caught a frown in my peripheral vision from Mama Fang.

"Not yet. Galina and Tanya spoke to her. She's freeing up her schedule to get here before Tanya's birthday bash if at all possible," Nika said. Nika and I work together and we really only answer to Elder Senka, but Galina continually tries to bring us both to heel.

"I will inform Mother of the details," Galina said, right on cue.

"Of course," I said.

"He said he would be back," Tanya said. "Tomorrow, to look for the demon."

"We'll have to see what he does, dear heart. He's only human," she said. Oh, that's the direction? Wrong choice, Mama, wrong choice. She really hadn't figured it out. Or was attempting to ignore the facts in hope that they would go away. Her little girl, who was also the basis of her personal power, had changed, drastically, in the course of five minutes. And those changes were still coming.

Decades ago, as a young girl, I traveled by train with my family out West on a winter trip. As we passed through the Rockies, the conductor pointed out an avalanche sliding down the side of one vast peak not overly far from our tracks. He turned to me with a wink and said, "Little lady, if you ever find yourself caught in an avalanche, don't try to fight it. It will crush you. Instead, try to float on it or sort of swim with it."

We were in the beginnings of an avalanche and Mama was fighting it. Nika and I were gonna sail a boat over the top of this one. My blonde friend caught my eye and winked.

"Well, Tanya. Lydia reports the police officer is okay and the good doctor has pronounced you fit. Perhaps it is time you settled in for the day, hmm?" Galina suggested.

"Okay," Tanya said, back to looking demure. She agreed much, much too quickly. Galina eyed her for a moment, but she was the very essence of innocence when she looked up at her mother.

"Come on T, let's go settle in. I'll do your nails while Nika tells us about *your* personal cop," I said, smiling at Tanya without a glance Galina's way. I grabbed Tanya's hand and pulled her toward her quarters, catching Nika's eye. The three of us took off, leaving a frowning Galina behind.

Tanya has a huge room on the second floor, with its own private patio garden on the top of the conservatory space. It's basically my second bedroom, mine and Nika's. We've spent many, many days with Tanya. Not all, but many. Vampires are at least as social as humans, usually more so, although how we socialize is maybe different from the stock species. Touch and contact are often part and parcel of our connections.

Once inside, we changed into sleepwear and I broke out the nail care supplies. Tanya sat cross-legged, her left hand draped on my knee while I removed her old polish. Our nails extend when we fight, becoming true claws, and it's hell on manicures. Hers were cracked and flaking.

"So... Nika?" Tanya asked. Nika lifted her head, ready to speak, but I held up a hand.

"Nope. Not yet. First, you maybe want to tell us what you're feeling?" I asked. She looked reluctant. "Tanya, you're speaking again. Hello, fifteen years?"

She met my gaze, then looked away. "He saved me. Then I attacked him and he saved me again. I think he touched my heart," she said. I smirked and her eyes narrowed. "No Lydia, I mean it. He literally touched my heart when he took out that piece of silver. It was like a big shock."

"Wait, you're saying he reached into your open wound and literally touched your heart?" I asked.

"He reached in and grabbed the shard of silver. I think one of his fingers brushed my actual heart. I felt a shock. I think he did too," she said.

"What happened after that?" I asked.

"It stopped me from feeding on him. Probably just in time," she said, eyes going off to the side.

"Maybe, maybe not. But you stopped. That was *your* decision. He could have punched you in the head and you could have just ignored it. You needed blood. I saw what was on the floor. You, yourself, lost more blood than most Darkkin could and still function. And you only took a portion of his, nowhere near what you lost," I said.

"But I'm fine, Lydia. Better than fine," she said.

"Exactly my point, my dear," I said, deciding to change topics. "So how did it taste? Your first live blood in fifteen years?"

Her eyes got wide. "Like no other blood I've ever had. Live or bagged."

"Well, it has been a while," Nika said.

"No, Nika. I've had blood so newly donated that the donor was still being bandaged when I drank it. People have brought me flavors of blood from all over the world. Nothing tasted like his," she said, frowning.

"So your boy toy has super blood," I said, picking through the reds in her collection of fingernail polish. Cliché, yes, but it seemed right. I picked a deep red.

"He's not my boy toy," she protested, suddenly crestfallen. "He doesn't even like me."

I looked at Nika, giving her a little head tilt, while taking Tanya's hand in mine.

"Oh, but he does, dear one. That's why he was so mad and hurt when you called him a liar," the blonde telepath said.

"He's mad at me?" Tanya said.

"Well, he was when he left. Which is why I know he likes you. You wouldn't get that level of emotional response if he didn't care about your opinion," Nika said.

"But now he's mad," she protested, looking down at the deep, blood red I was painting onto the nails of her left hand.

"He'll get over it," I said with a shrug. "He'll remember how hot you looked and forget all about his anger."

"That's actually really true. Men are simple, visual creatures, Tanya. They are easily overwhelmed by good looks," Nika said.

"Well, he's pretty good looking too, don't you think?" our vampire princess asked.

"He is. And he has amazing eyes," I agreed, watching carefully.

"I know, right?" she exclaimed. Her hand twitched, just a small tremor really. On Tanya, that was the equivalent of a regular person jerking their hand right out of mine. Someone was pretty hyped up. "So you think he'll come back, to, ah, hunt that demon thing—the Hellbourne?"

"He strikes me as a young man of his word. I would expect him to follow through with his intent to protect you," I said.

Nika nodded. "He went away mad but still determined to hunt the thing," she said.

"And it's very dangerous. I never even saw that thing till it had already shot me," Tanya said.

"I don't think they can sneak up on him, Tanya. He tracked that thing like a bloodhound, right through the club. And he's done this many times. He's probably no more in danger from this demon than from our own security guys," I said. Her head snapped up, staring into my eyes. Then she was gone, the door left swinging open as the wind of her passage left lilac and jasmine notes hanging in the air.

We tracked her down, *moving* to keep up. Found her on the main floor, standing in front of a startled Vadim and Arkady.

"And you will tell Mr. Deckert not to hurt him if he shows up here?" she was asking. Actually, it seemed more like a demand.

"Yes, Tanya. I will convey that message to Deckert when he comes on shift," the big vampire said. Him in his snakeskin vest, staring down at the compact beauty in white and pink footie pajamas. "Although he doesn't likely know where we live."

"He'll find us. He is very resourceful," Nika said. Vadim nodded at her words but Arkady just stared at her. Nika and I wore more abbreviated sleepwear than Tanya, and everyone in Demidova central knew Arkady had a bit of a thing for our telepath.

"Satisfied?" I asked. Tanya held Vadim's eyes for a moment, then turned to me and nodded. Nika grabbed her hand and led her away. I waited till they were on the staircase, talking about what Nika had meant about the cop's resourcefulness.

"A word of caution? Make sure the day crew understands how important that cop's health is. I think it is safe to say it is literally a matter of life and death... theirs. And you," I said, turning to Arkady, "don't even glare in that particular human's direction."

"You can't think she has Chosen?" Vadim asked.

"I can and I do."

Upstairs, we got our excited princess calmed, talking about boys and kissing and boys, as the sky outside began to lighten. The automatic shades slid down over the windows and gradually the three of us succumbed to the pressure of the new day, falling into our normal deep slumber.

Sudden movement brought me awake all at once. Tanya was sitting upright in her massive king bed, and then she was gone—again. Outside, night was falling.

It took me longer to track her through the house, but her angry voice was as clear as a bell. She was in the back of the ground floor, standing in the door of the security office. She had a hand on each side of the doorframe, her nails extended and driven deep into the splintering wood.

"Who hurt him?" she hissed at Deckert. I smelled urine as I got closer... and fear. Lots of good old human fear.

There were five heavily armed, highly trained ex-special ops types in that office, and they were all smart enough to realize that their immediate death was standing in the doorway.

"What happened?" I asked, loud enough to at least get the daytime security chief's attention. Deckert was a retired Marine (never say ex-Marine, trust me). Like all the other human security staff, he was battle hardened and highly experienced. But Deckert took the whole confident, unruffled thing to lofty new levels for a human. We liked to joke that Tanya was the only born vampire, but Deckert was born with the mind of one. He was sweating.

"The individual that Security Chief Vadim warned us about, Officer Chris Gordon, entered the rear compound over the wall and apprehended an individual we failed to detect, despite Vadim's warning and description. He then proceeded to conduct some form of arcane exorcism ritual and the other intruder was left dead. During his altercation with the intruder, Officer Gordon scraped his check on the stone of the patio. To our knowledge, that is the only wound he sustained," Deckert said, eyes alternating between me and Tanya. The other four had moved their eyes to me, refusing to risk looking at the angry death angel in front of me.

"Oh, and it bled a little, right? The cheek?" I asked, understanding blooming in my head.

"Just a little. He did not require any first aid and would not stay. He said he had to help a child with a problem tonight. A demonic problem," Deckert said.

I put my hand on Tanya's arm, feeling the steel hardness of it relax to merely oak density.

"He is alright?" she asked, her voice much, much less harsh than seconds before.

"He bounced right up in front of all my guys like he was ready take us all on. Then Sykes brought Apollo out and the damned dog just lay down on this cop's feet like a lap dog. Wagged his damn tail," Deckert said.

"Apollo likes him?" Tanya asked. By now the guys had shifted from fear of her to astonishment at her speech.

"Of course the dog liked him. He's like a damned guard dog himself. All purple puppy dog eyes," I said.

Tanya giggled, just a little. "Lydia, you're being facetious," she protested, yet she was smiling at my words.

Deckert's eyes widened at the abrupt change in our princess, but he wisely kept his mouth shut.

"So he's helping out a child?" Tanya asked him.

"He got a text while I was talking to him. He didn't like it. I told him he needed to be here for when Galina woke up, but he refused. Said he had to leave but that you all could likely track him down if you needed to," Deckert said.

"What was your impression, Mr. Deckert?" I asked.

"Kid has bal... guts. He scrambled over our wall way too easy and he's got good ground fighting skills. Ran a background check; he comes up spotless. First name is actually Christian. Got very high marks in the police academy. Also, he's not easily intimidated, ma'am. "

"No, Mr. Deckert, he's not," I said.

"He fought well?" Tanya asked.

"Ahem, I have the footage here, ma'am, if you like," one of the other security guys suggested, pointing at the CCTV system.

"Oh yes, I would like that very much," Tanya said. Then she turned to Deckert. "I am sorry I was so abrupt with you and your men, Mr. Deckert. I smelled *his* blood and thought he'd been harmed," she said.

"Ah, well, we were very careful to follow Vadim's instructions regarding Officer Gordon, ma'am," Deckert said, clearly confused but adapting.

Tanya nodded, then turned to the one guard who had pissed himself, his khaki pants wet down the inside of both legs.

"I am sorry to frighten you, Samuel. I will buy you new pants. Maybe in black or navy blue this time?" she asked, eyebrows raised. Was that a joke?

The guy by the monitors snorted. "You might need to get those for all of us, ma'am. I wasn't far behind Sam myself. Here's the footage," he said. My suddenly talkative ward moved smoothly over to the bank of monitors, the men hastily making space for the girl in footie pajamas.

Deckert waited till she was engrossed in the action, then turned to me with raised eyebrows.

"Mr. Gordon saved Tanya from that demon last night. She was grossly wounded and fed from him. He promised her he would come back today and see if he could catch that thing," I explained. "As you've noticed, she's decided to talk to us again."

Tanya sniffed. "Well, of course I had to talk. I had to speak to Christian," she said, not looking away from the monitor. "Oh, that's some kind of modified armbar," she said, hands darting to the keyboard to back up the footage and roll it again.

"The thing didn't seem to feel pain, ma'am. He was obviously trying to be real fast, then he held up his arm and that bird thing came and it was all over," another guard, Benson, said.

"Bird thing?" Tanya asked.

"Something supernatural. It just kind of *popped* in, grabbed something from his hand, then popped out. Huge. As big as a hang glider," Benson said, pointing to the screen. I found I had moved myself closer to see, and the images defied logic.

Tanya turned to me, eyes wide. "Lydia, do you think that was an angel?"

"Seemed like a really big, smokey eagle or hawk, Miss Tanya. There was this kinda sound, like a note on a bell or crystal or something. But it didn't strike me as angelic. Not that I'd be a good judge," Benson said.

"Benson was there when it happened," Deckert explained.

Tanya turned to me but didn't speak. She didn't need to.

"Yes, we will track him down. Somehow," I said.

The guys were all exchanging glances but none of them dared comment.

"Good. I want to see him," she said, her tone brooking no argument.

Why did I suddenly think we were all going to be seeing him—a lot. Fifteen years of silence and it all changed in one night, in less than five minutes. She was like a whole different person, like she had grown in years over the course of hours.

Demon hunter or cop or whatever, there was way more to this guy than anyone knew. But deep down in my gut, I did *know* that whatever we found out in the days ahead, it was gonna be huge.

Growing Pains

Raising teenagers is hard work. But what if your kid was touched by God?

Alex Gordon pulled into the farmhouse driveway and shut off the engine of his F-150. As he stepped out, his left foot went into a puddle of spring melt, almost up to the very bottom of the laces. Quickly yanking it clear, he waited for any sign of icy wetness inside his sock, but the Sno Seal waterproofing he worked into all his boots held firm.

He stamped his feet hard on the slab of sandstone just before the little porch, wiped his boots on the welcome mat, then again on the old floor rug just inside the door. The mud room entry was a shambles of boots, sneakers, and haphazardly hung jackets. He paused and listened to the old house. A slight hiss and rhythmic metallic thudding brought him into the kitchen to the Fisher wood stove, whose door was just slightly ajar and swinging as the well-fed fire inside drew air in steady gusts.

Kid fed the stove when he got home, then left the door open to get the fire up to heat. Alex latched the stove door shut. A glance at the counter showed lidless jars of peanut butter and Smucker's grape jelly, a purple-coated table knife laying across the mouth of the jelly jar. The bread loaf bag had been closed and wire tied, but none of the sandwich fixings had made it back to their rightful places in the old farm kitchen.

Alex moved slowly into the living room, immediately spotting a crumb-strewn plate on the coffee table, next to a familiar book bag. An empty glass with a coating of milk at the bottom stood next to the plate. No kid though. Again, he paused and listened. Silence, then suddenly a dull thwack, coming from the bathroom or else just outside the bathroom. He moved into the little half-bath off the family room and looked out the window at the sideyard.

A kid. Mid-teens, jeans and Timberland work boots, worn t-shirt selling the virtues of Mattock's Feed and Stock. The shirt had either shrunk over countless washings or else the kid had grown again, because the well-worn cotton clung to a tightly muscled torso that flexed as it powered a heavy splitting maul up and over broad shoulders, then down into a big chunk of sugar maple. That's right, Len had mentioned that he was going to drop the ancient maple on the side of the house before *it* could drop *on* the house. Len had bucked it up into big three-foot diameter rounds and now the kid was going to town on it.

Spring in Northern New York was still pretty cool, but the air steamed around the fifteen-yearold, and a good sized pile of split maple indicated that he'd been working hard for a while.

Reading sign was a habit trained into Alex Gordon, first by his father, then by the Corps (reinforced by the North Korean army), and honed by decades living on an active farm. Whether you were tracking a sheep-killing coyote through St. Lawrence County forest, an enemy soldier through foreign lands, or an upset teen through a farm house, sign was sign. It was interpreting it that counted.

Outside the window, Alex's grandson, Christian Gordon, moved around the knotty two-foot hank of maple that had started out being a full foot wider in diameter. Close cut, almost military-length brown hair framed a tanned face that looked boy-next-door until the kid lifted his head to reveal eyes a shade of violet rarely found in the human iris. A deep, angry frown and narrowed gaze lasered the troublesome round of wood that was clearly putting up a hell of a fight. Multiple blade marks on the top of the wood indicated that Chris had found himself a knotted nightmare, but the kid wasn't letting it go.

Taking a step back, Chris wound the maul back up behind him and slammed it down in a hard arc that would have rung the bell on any carnival strongman high-striker game in the state. It only succeeded in wedging the maul into the top of the log. Clearly undeterred, Chris stepped forward, bent at the knees, grabbed the maul handle tight up near the head, and powered both the ax and attached log up behind his right shoulder.

He took a step to the right, lined up with another yet-untouched round of heavy old wood that he was using as a chopping block, and brought the ax and log over his shoulder, upside down so that the back of the head hit the block first, momentum driving the log down further onto the blade. It was a technique that Alex had taught Chris himself, and it was usually just the medicine for a reluctant log. Sometimes though, the log was just too gnarled.

The maul was now buried almost to the top of its head in the tough wood and Chris pulled the whole thing back, swinging the forty or fifty pound bundle up over his shoulder and slamming it down again. Alex could see the maul was now truly jammed deep in the unyielding maple and the kid was huffing and puffing with the effort, face twisted in disbelief and anger.

"Shit," Alex muttered, hurrying out of the bathroom, back through the living room and kitchen and out the back door. Jumping straight into a mammoth splitting job after just a quick snack wasn't Chris... unless he was mad or upset or both. Now he was frustrated on top of all that and Alex knew he had to hurry if he was going to save the handle of his good splitting maul.

"Hold up a sec, Chris. Let me grab some wedges and a sledge. We'll double team that SOB."

Chris looked at him, clearly and completely annoyed with everything, then swung the knotted mess back up. "No, son, you'll—" was as far as Alex got before the ax came down. Tired from the two previous heavy-duty swings, on top of a half-hour of splitting, Chris missed hitting the block in the center. Instead, he hit too far forward, the handle of the maul connecting with the sharp edge of the block, snapping with a loud, clear crack.

"I'll replace it," Chris said after staring at the broken maul for three full seconds.

"Yes you will. You'll get the wedge and sledge and get the head free, then you'll put a new handle on it," Alex said evenly. "You'll also pick up your mess in the house."

"I was always going to do that," Chris said with a grimace.

"But you're not doing any of it right now," Alex said, his tone more that his words catching Chris's attention.

"What am I doing instead?" Chris asked, frowning.

"You're taking a trip with me. We gotta check out a place south of Newcomb. Disparius. Tiny, eye-blink of a town in the mountains," Alex said, gesturing toward the house.

"What's up with Disparius... which sounds like desperate?" Chris asked.

"It is—desperate. Little town on the Upper Hudson River. Old garnet mining community. Pretty economically desolate now. I gotta a call from a guy I know. Seems the place has gotten really hinky lately."

"Like what?" Chris asked, broken maul handle dangling forgotten in his hand.

"My friend has lived near there for years. Place was always a bit run down. Now, though, it's got a real nasty vibe to it. He hunts all around there, says the woods around the town are empty of animals. Says the people he knows there have all gotten mean and very strange. Also, his daughter is sensitive. She won't go through the town, even in a car. Says evil lives there."

"So when we going?" Chris asked, dropping the handle.

"Now. Two fly fishermen just disappeared in the area. Got that from my same friend, who runs the regional ranger office in Warrensburg."

Just like that, the annoyed, angst-filled teen was gone and the young man that Alex secretly and only to himself called God's Soldier was staring at him with violet eyes. Turning toward the house, Chris trotted toward the back door. "I'll grab some fetishes and my go bag, Gramps. Meet you at the truck."

Alex followed his grandson at a brisk walk, leaving the extra hustle to the youth. Entering his bedroom, Alex pulled his own go bag from the closet and double-checked that the water bottles in the side pocket were full. Then he went to his bedside table and fetched his Wilson custom combat .45 and cleared its chamber. Normal carry was chamber hot, safety locked. Carrying in demon country was the exact opposite. His right leg still bore the scar when a demonic entity clicked off his safety and tripped the sear, sending a big hollowpoint along the outside of his thigh, all from a holstered gun. Luckily, the pistol had jammed in the holster or the follow-up rounds would have been much worse.

Belting the gun on, he added two double magazine belt carriers on his left side, then pulled his Carhartt work jacket over the whole kit and caboodle. A quick double check assured him that his mountain lion fetish was hanging around his neck, which was way more important than the gun. Grabbing the go pack, he headed for the door, meeting his foreman, Len, who was on his way in.

"Need any backup?" Len asked after a quick glance at the pack.

"I'm thinking no, but don't be too far from the phone just in case we need to call for the Calvary."

"Air cav maybe," Len said with a grunt. "He's already in the truck, game face on," he added, thumbing back over his shoulder.

"I think he came home bothered by something, but he tucks it away when duty calls."

"Kid would make a hell of a Marine," Len said for maybe the thousandth time.

Clapping his old second-in-command on the shoulder, Alex headed out to the truck.

They were thirty minutes into the drive, almost halfway to Tupper Lake and already inside the Adirondack Park, before Alex took a stab at the elephant in the truck.

"So... want to talk about it?"

Chris turned from looking out his window, eyebrows up for just a split second before he figured out the question's context. He turned to look straight ahead, shoulders slumping a bit.

Alex waited, knowing things would either come at their own pace or not come at all.

It was almost a full minute before the silence broke.

"That dickwad Craig Schnell is going out on Lisa Guyette. She doesn't have a clue."

Fifteen years old is a time when most boys are really beginning to pay attention to the opposite sex, even demon-hunting, Heaven-favored boys. Maybe especially those, although Alex only knew of one.

"Do any of her girlfriends know?" Alex asked, wracking his brain to remember more about this Lisa other than her name had come up before. Chris didn't have friends, especially girls. Much too great a danger to the individual, too big a draw for Hell's hunters here on earth. But he could admire from afar.

"Who knows. It's some girl from Parishville, I think. Saw them in his car out behind the bus maintenance building. Mr. Harris sent me out to get some new weight plates that got dropped off there."

Chris spent an hour in the school's weight room almost every afternoon, an arrangement that Alex had made with the school's football and strength training coach.

"How do you know she's from Parishville?" Alex asked. Chris didn't socialize with his *own* schoolmates, so how did he recognize a girl from another school?

"I'm pretty sure she's a football cheerleader."

Football was Chris's only sport, and he only played it to build his speed, reflexes, and ability to tackle. The other coaches were always pressuring the kid to try additional sports, but other than a short experiment with wrestling, football was it. Some of his *volunteer* trainers could provide way more grappling arts training, but there was nothing like tackling a bigger, stronger runner to hone his skills in that department. But he really had to be paying attention to girls if he remembered a specific cheerleader.

"So you're the only one who knows?" Alex asked. He got a nod in response. "Can't really tell anyone because you don't hang with them and they wouldn't trust you, right?" he asked, sort of talking it through out loud. Another nod.

"Okay. I'll take care of it," Alex said, carefully keeping his eyes on the road.

In his peripheral vision, he saw Chris snap around to look at him.

"What?" The tone was clear disbelief.

"I said I'll take care of it."

"But, but, why… how… Gramps, what are you talking about?" Chris sputtered.

"You can't intervene, can't show favorites, can't make friends. Lisa is someone you think well of, so I'll take care of it," Alex said, enjoying himself immensely.

"What would you even do?"

"Just a word here or there," he said, going for mysterious.

Chris was quiet for a moment or two. "Oh. You'll mention it to the guys and they'll pull him over, maybe with Lisa in the car, maybe with the other one. Drop a comment or something," he said, working it through. The *guys* were a handful of Saint Lawrence County deputy sheriffs, some of the only people clued in about his grandson. Damn, that kid was quick.

"Something like that," Alex admitted, still hoping to retain some of the mystery of being Chris's problem-solver.

When he was honest with himself, Alex could admit that he loved being a grandfather more than anything else in his life. First the military, then work, either as a dairy farmer or during the period he had run the farm supply company, had taken massive amounts of his life, leaving him with far fewer memories of his family than he should have. If he could do it over, he never would have traded work for family life. His only son had grown up and left in the blink of an eye, starting a family of his own. Then suddenly they too were gone. Only Chris had survived. Being Gramps to God's chosen soldier was a gift he refused to squander. The farm was still a work-intensive bastard but with Len and his farmhands, it pretty much ran itself. Times like this, missions of good versus evil, with his grandson, were what he lived for. Because, soon enough, this too would be gone.

"Thanks, Gramps," Chris said, turning to look at him.

"No problem," he said, poker faced. Inside, he rejoiced at the confidence Chris had in him.

"So what's up with these fishermen?" Chris asked a minute later. School drama solved, at least for now, they got down to shop talk.

"Couple of guys up from the city. They've been here before, on guided float trips out of North Creek. This time, they went on their own. Never showed up downstream. The En-Con guys out of Warrensburg put out a call for people to help with a search and rescue starting at first light."

Alex Gordon was well-known across the northern part of New York State as a search and rescue resource. Success at hunting enemy soldiers as the leader of a Marine Raider Platoon in Korea had translated to being highly successful at hunting lost hunters, hikers, and tourists in the vast Adirondack Park.

"Let me guess—their float trip should have taken them through Disparius?" Chris asked.

"Correct. But Sean Sears, the local DEC guy, says that the locals weren't really helpful, or even attempting to be helpful," Alex said. Chris didn't respond. He glanced at his grandson. The boy was frozen, eyes wide, mouth open, staring straight ahead. Alex immediately pulled the truck over to the shoulder of the road.

"Chris? Chris?" he asked, shaking the boy. It took two shakes before the eyes blinked and the mouth shut.

"Shit!" Chris said, blinking at his gramps, who ignored the bad language. Then the boy was rummaging in the glove compartment, pulling out an old receipt for an oil change. Further scrabbles in the glove box produced a pencil and then the kid was drawing, sketching like a man possessed.

"What are you doing? What happened to you?" Alex asked, baffled.

"I don't know. It was a vision. I saw the fishermen, saw them tied up," Chris said, staring with slightly wild eyes into Alex's. Somehow, the pencil kept going, almost by itself.

They both looked down at the picture, which Alex was amazed to see was really, really good. He looked back up and met Chris's own astonished gaze. "I don't think it's even... me," the kid said.

They both looked back down, ready at last to focus on the picture's details.

Two men, bound back-to-back and slung upside down by their ankles, suspended over what looked like a cast iron pot. They wore recognizable fishing vests, a few feathered lures visible. Figures in robes and cowls surrounded them, a ridiculously large knife in one male figure's hand.

Overhead, a round ball appeared to cast light through what had to be a stained glass window made colorless by the white paper and pencil.

"It's a full moon tonight," Chris said, pointing out the windshield on the other side of his gramps at the yellow orb hanging just over the eastern tree line.

"But this moon is really high, based on the angle," Alex said, taking the picture and turning it.

"I don't think this has happened yet," Chris said. "At least, that's the feeling I have."

"And I know where this is!" Alex said. "Sean described some of the town to me. There's an abandoned church that someone may be living in. That looks an awful lot like a stained glass window to me."

"How do we find the church?"

"Sean said you can't miss it. Right on the main road through town," Alex replied, putting the truck back in gear and easing back out onto the road. "Gotta get there in time."

"I think we will," his grandson said, a strange confidence in his voice.

Twelve minutes later, they crested a hill, spying the lights of Tupper Lake below them. Twenty-five minutes after that, they were in Long Lake, turning left onto Route 28 South, the Roosevelt-Marcy trail that Teddy Roosevelt took in the middle of a September night in 1901 when President McKinley died from complications of a gunshot wound.

Another forty-eight miles and they spotted the tiny sign for Disparius. Slowing the Ford, Alex kept his eyes forward as he spoke. "So, just like we discussed. We'll drive by the church building, then find a place to park and sneak back. Recon the situation and then I'll call my ranger contact on my cell phone, got it?" Alex asked, holding up the Motorola flip phone he had let Chris talk him into buying. Chris reached over and took the phone, opening the lid and looking at the display.

"Ah, Gramps... no signal. Probably no cell tower out this way," Chris said.

"Shit," Alex said. "The plan has already met its maker."

"So we need to scout a landline while we're looking things over. Call your buddy from that phone, then see about getting these guys free," Chris said, tapping the useless cell phone against the drawing on his lap.

"Remember, you deal with the demon, I got the rank and file," Alex said, adrenaline making his hands shake a little. A small, whitish, ill-kept church appeared on their left and Alex slowed even further.

Tiny and badly in need of paint, the house-of-God-shaped building felt entirely wrong to Alex. Like it was befouled.

Chris studied it intently and Alex snuck as many looks at it as he could without crashing the pickup, then the little building was gone and they were around a bend in the road. Alex drove another quarter mile, past several houses and a couple shack-like hovels that he suspected were also houses, before finding a road that connected onto the route they were on. He made the side turn and parked the pickup, showed Chris where he was hiding the keys, then finally double-checked his holstered .45.

Chris hopped out first and looked around at the moonlit forest that pressed in on them from both sides. The land rose and fell sharply, the road they had come in on twisting to match its rugged contours.

Exchanging nods, they turned and trudged along the side of the main road, back toward the church.

The first house they passed didn't appear to have any telephone wires coming off the overhead line, but the next one up did. That one had the soft glow of a light coming from one dirty window.

Alex scouted around the property, posting Chris in the shadow of a small cedar tree while he studied the place. No dog dishes, run lines, or other signs of canine habitation, which was good. The house was a dump, but the wood piles were neat and orderly, comprising perhaps four full cords, he thought.

Moving up to a window, he eased up until his right eye just peeked through the lower corner. Nothing. A jumbled living area, old recliner draped with a blue blanket, television dark on its stand, single lamp on an end table dimly lighting the place. Through a doorway, he saw what might have been a kitchen.

He moved over to the almost-paint-free wooden porch and stepped carefully, as close to the wall as he could get. The wood creaked and groaned slightly, but not enough for most people to hear, or so he judged. Working carefully, he peered though the mullioned glass outer door and the single pane of the main door. Nothing. Empty kitchen, dirty and ill-kept like the rest of the place. A small red light glowed on the counter. Base station for a cord-free phone. Bingo.

The doors were both unlocked and he opened them with truly stellar stealth and care. He glanced at Chris and gave him three quick military hand signals. Watch, listen, and cover this area. He wanted his kid sharp while he was in the house. Chris made a clear *Okay, I understand* signal back. Then there was nothing for it but to get on with it.

The kitchen floor was linoleum, old and even dirtier than the rest of the place. He moved with a deliberate, slow step-by-step motion, pulling his foot back if he felt give in the floor or heard the slightest creak. Despite all his military training and hunting experience, it was fatherhood that had provided the skill to move without waking a sleeping baby or alert a homeowner.

Five steps brought him to the counter. The base station was empty, the receiver missing in action. Frustrated, he made a slow, deliberate visual sweep of the kitchen, then the portion of the living room he could see. Nothing. Wait, what was that? A nub of something plastic was visible poking up from the recliner cushion. He leaned forward. Maybe. Six more slow steps brought him just into the living room. Enough of the plastic was now visible for him to see part of a keypad. He looked left and right, paused to listen, and, not hearing anything, stepped lightly into the room. The floor creaked and something exploded out from under the chair.

His gun was out of the holster, his left hand racking the action before he realized the furry missile that blurred by him was a cat. He froze, listening. Now would be when the monster would leap at him, at least based on the horror movies Chris was curiously okay with watching. Nothing happened.

He moved forward and grabbed the phone. It hummed with a dial tone when he pressed send. Perfect. Turning it off, he retraced his steps, hyper alert for attack, but nothing happened. The house was truly empty.

An orange marmalade cat hissed at him from under the kitchen table as he stepped out onto the porch. Chris was exactly where he left him and Alex could almost see the relief when his grandkid saw him. He clicked the safety on and holstered the Wilson as he moved to Chris's position.

"Wireless. We don't have to be inside."

"But we won't get more than a couple hundred feet from the house before it loses the signal,"Chris said.

"Let's recon the church, then we'll pull back here and make the call."

"Roger that," Chris said, completely serious.

They moved down the road, slipping off into the ditch on the same side as the church. Up close, the thing felt really, really wrong and all of Alex's instincts screamed at him to get out of there. A glance at Chris showed that his grandson felt the place too, probably with more detail than Alex ever would, but his expression was locked down and determined. A soldier's face.

The building loomed closer and Alex became aware of voices, chanting voices. He signaled Chris to split left and that he would take the right. Rally at the back. Chris nodded, disappearing into the moonlit shadows.

Light flickered in both the regular windows and the stained glass windows, obviously flame, either candle or torch. Chris's drawing had both in it. A chill shivered up Alex's spine. His grandson was now suddenly getting visions of demons, and all evidence pointed to them being real.

The voices inside got louder near the back, about where he judged that the original sanctuary would be. No one was outside.

The building was small, and it took just a few minutes to reconnoiter his side of it. He found Chris waiting at the back. "Nothing," Chris whispered.

"Me either. Total absence of security on this operation," Alex whispered back.

Chris held up a hand and waved it about, eyebrows raised. Good point. They were deep in the Adirondacks on a very low volume road in a nowhere hamlet in the dark of night.

"I did peek through a window. I saw two men tied up but couldn't see their faces. Something like ten or twelve people. Wearing robes. Like the vision," Chris said.

"Let's make the call."

Chris nodded but pointed up at the rising moon. His point was clear. The clock ticked onward.

They scooted back down the road till the handheld receiver picked up the base station, then Alex called his ranger contact. "What do you mean? You asked for help and we helped. They're tied up in some weird occult ritual," Chris heard his grandfather say. "What did you expect? You know what we do, right? No, no, beyond search and rescue. The other thing?" A pause to listen. "Yes that. Why? Because you said you got a creepy vibe, that's why. Your vibe was right." Another pause. "As long as we can, but if we think things are going pear shaped, we'll have to act. Right, then hurry up and get here."

Alex hung up and just looked at the phone for a moment. "Didn't believe you?" Chris asked.

"Actually, I think he did. He just didn't *want* to believe."

"How many cops and rangers and stuff know about me?" Chris asked, shifting side-to-side on his feet.

"Enough. Cops see things. They're trained to only report information that is evidential and verifiable, but they still see a lot of really weird stuff. And they talk to each other. So it might seem odd to you that the people you would least expect to believe sometimes do. Not all of them, but enough," Alex said. "Now, let's get eyes on the situation and observe. No action unless we have to. Sean is on his way and is calling one of the state troopers who covers this area. We should hold on till then."

"Okay, but I don't think there's a lot more time left till this all goes down," Chris said, looking up at the height of the moon.

They moved stealthily around to the window that Chris had used earlier. It was next to a side door near the back of the church. Alex carefully tested the knob to see if they could get in if they had to. It turned smoothly and the door wasn't bolted.

Through the window, he could see two figures tied back-to-back, lying on the plank wood floor in front of the altar. Figures in brown and black robes, which mostly looked like old blankets, stood chanting across from a lone figure whose robe seemed more legitimate. That one stood, arms tucked into sleeves, head bowed as if in prayer.

"What do you think?" Alex asked.

"The single figure is a Hellbourne. The rest are just twisted people."

"Hellbourne being a demon that's taken over a human?" Alex whispered back. "Like the *one*?"

"A demon who has pushed out the human completely. Like a hermit crab taking over another one's shell. Like the one from *that* night."

"How do you know?" Alex asked. He didn't disbelieve Chris, but he was endlessly curious.

"I can literally feel him. Like his presence is pressing on a membrane around my mind. Like before."

"Can he feel you?"

"I don't think so. That's why I survived the attack. I think your fetish keeps you hidden, too," Chris said.

"Is it the same one? From that night?"

"I don't think so. But I remember that it was faster and stronger than dad or Marcus."

"Which means faster and stronger than you," Alex said, worry rising.

"Yes, but this is what you've been training me for. If I can get hands on him, he's mine."

"I think it's too soon," Alex said. "And you don't know if you can actually do anything."

"But here's the thing, Gramps. I do. I absolutely know that if I get hands on him, he's mine," Chris said with a surety that Alex had never heard before.

The chanting rose to a crescendo then suddenly stopped.

"It's starting," Chris said, moving toward the door.

"Wait. Let me look first," Alex said, leaning back up to the window for a peek. A rope was now over the exposed rafter beams of the cathedral ceiling, one end tied to the fishermen, the other being dragged up by four big men. The leader had pulled his hands apart and out of his sleeves. A massive black blade with twisting shapes carved on it was in his left hand.

"It's happening," Alex said, moving in front of Chris and pulling his .45. The safety snicked off as his left hand twisted the knob, Chris close behind him. He rushed through as the door opened, bringing his pistol up, front sight covering the knife-wielding Hellbourne.

As he felt Chris push through behind him, he caught motion out of the right corner of his eyes. A man with an ax was rushing at him, but the four rope pullers were in the way. The gun tracked to the new threat and fired twice, almost on its own.

The ax man fell forward, blood spraying out his back. Then all of Alex's muscles locked up tight.

"What have we got he..." the Hellbourne started to say but stopped as Chris moved into position in front of his grandfather, his left hand reaching back to touch Alex's own left arm. The paralysis disappeared and Alex swung his sights back onto the Hellbourne while trying to keep one eye on the thing's disciples.

The Hellbourne was frozen, eyes wide as it took in Chris. Then it smiled an inhuman smile, somehow stretching the mouth of the body it wore in a completely wrong attempt at a grin.

"Unexpected," it said. Then it brought the knife around in a blur of motion.

"Shoot it," Chris said, his tone absolutely certain. The gun seemed to go off on its own, but the Hellbourne wasn't there when the bullet passed through the spot it had occupied. The thing was really fast, shifting to his left in an eyeblink. He missed with his second shot as it moved left again.

But Alex Gordon had seen a lot of combat and had fired thousands of rounds from guns just like this one at all kinds of targets, living or not. He twitched the barrel toward the Hellbourne, then brought it back a half inch before firing. The thing had watched his gun barrel and flickered to his right, but the half inch back was just right and this time, bullet met demon. Just barely. It hit the monster's left arm, the big bullet flinging the arm back, the knife flying away.

It immediately twisted back toward his left but this time Chris hit it, having started his rush while the knife was still moving. Its good right arm swung up, fast and powerful, but his grandson was already inside the arc of the swing. Instead of a fist, it was the inside of the elbow that hit the teen, the power enough to knock him about, but his own arm had time to get hooked under the Hellbourne's right one and his other arm pulled down on the wounded limb. Alex knew what would happen next; he'd seen it a hundred times. Sure enough, Chris's hip tucked into the demon's midsection and the boy twisted up, over and down, executing a judo hip toss that, if not picture perfect, was still extremely fast and effective.

The demon landed on its head and shoulders, already squirming to get free, but Chris must have begun his thing, the thing he called *pushing power*, because the Hellbourne body went rigid, back arched up. Chris had control of the good right arm and had the joint locked with the palm of his left hand on it, his full body weight holding the demon down. Alex noticed that his grandson's eyes were closed. Black *stuff* began to bubble up out the the actual skin of the elbow, collecting and pooling around Chris's left hand, moving about like it had a life of its own.

The boy suddenly pulled away and stood up, the body slumping lifeless to the floor. Left hand encased in viscous oily-black crud, he lifted that arm and something like the mother of all chimes sounded, a single clear note that brought a fleeting perfect feeling that all was right. The rope slithered over the beam as the four men holding it let go, faces stunned.

The space above their heads was suddenly filled with a *presence,* a smoky, flapping, flying presence as big as a couch. Talons as long as a butter knife clutched Chris's upraised hand and the awesome flying thing pulled up and away. The black, squirming putrescence was now clutched in the talons of the bird's left foot and the big yellow beak lifted and screamed a victorious cry. The air above them collapsed and the smoky bird was gone.

The robed disciples were looking like they'd all been poleaxed, eyes unfocused as Alex moved his pistol barrel to cover them, his own gaze darting to Chris to make sure he was alright.

The kid looked tired but elated at the same time. He gave Alex a smile then turned his attention to the bound men. He reached to the small his back, under his hooded sweatshirt, and pulled out a short, viciously sharp blade from a horizontal sheath. Len's influence. The old Marine was usually covered in knives and that small of the back thing was his signature.

The blade made short work of the fishermen's bonds and Chris got them away from the residents and sitting up.

Rough boots sounded on the wooden steps outside and suddenly a dark green uniformed figure with a pump shotgun rushed in the open door.

"Glad you made it," Alex said.

Ranger Sears looked around the room, eyes taking in the missing fishermen, the empty body, the wounded axman and the robed figures. His gaze lingered for a moment on the purple-eyed teen, then he turned to Alex with raised eyebrows.

It took longer to tell the tale than it did to actually live it. Forty minutes later, Sean was satisfied, although the troopers and Warren county sheriff's deputies were still processing the scene.

"Kid's pretty special, huh?" Sean asked, both of them looking at his grandson, who sat in Alex's truck.

"That doesn't begin to cover it, Sean. Not even close."

"What's he doing, anyway?" Ranger Sears asked.

"I suspect he's studying. Got a Spanish quiz tomorrow... in like nine hours, and he's not great at it."

The veteran forest ranger turned to Alex, expression incredulous.

"He's pretty tickled though. That thing in there, it was like the one that killed my son, daughter-in-law, and my other grandson. And a fifteen-year-old boy just took it down and sent it back to Hell."

"If I hadn't felt that tone, or heard that, that... thing cry out in victory, I'd be thinking about wrestling you into a funny white jacket with no cuffs," Ranger Sears said.

"Glad you and Trooper Mousaw were handy when it happened, then," Alex said. "But you're the one who said this place gave you the heebie-jeebies."

The door of the pickup opened and both men looked up to see Chris getting out. "Ah Ranger Sears, I almost forgot. This is for you," the boy said, pulling a black cord and small blue dog-like figure from around his neck. The ranger could see another necklace still there, a feather and arrowhead, but then the hoody swallowed it back up.

"What's this?" Sears asked.

"I try to have extras on me when we do an exorcism. Afterward, we've found they act like repellant. It'll protect you," Chris said unsurely, glancing at his grandfather.

Alex fished his own lion figurine out from under his shirt.

"That's a coyote. Zuni carved," Chris said.

The ranger looked up at the boy, eyes surprised all over again.

"That's kinda odd. I had a coyote as a kid. Was hit by a truck and I helped the lady who rehabilitated it. Always had a soft spot for them since," Sears said.

"Funny, huh?" Alex asked with a grin.

Sears' look of disbelief changed to a grimace and he flicked a middle finger at the now-chuckling Alex. "You two need to hit the road. Someone's got a test tomorrow."

Chris looked chagrined. "Ugh, can't I stay home?"

"What would your grandmother have said to that?"

The teen didn't answer. Instead, he just sighed and turned to go.

"Chris?" Ranger Sears asked.

When the boy turned back, he found a big meaty hand held out. He grinned and shook it, then trudged back to the truck.

"Let me know if you ever, *ever* need help of any kind for that one," Sears said.

"Oh, don't worry. I'll call in every chip, favor, and debt if I ever need to."

"Good, now get out of here. We got this."

Five minutes later, they were pulling out onto the road they'd arrived on. "Gramps?" Chris asked suddenly.

"Yes Chris?"

"Do you think I'd make a good cop?"

"Oh, you'd make a great cop. Why?"

"I think that's what I want to be," Chris said.

"Oh, like a trooper or ranger?"

"Maybe. Or maybe in New York City."

"Well, it's good to have goals, Chris. It's good to have goals."

Under Heaven and Earth

There are more things...

"Okay Boy Scout, you're up," Ryan Cotter said, pointing at the campsite fire pit.

Keitan didn't much care for his tone. "What, you can't build a fire?" he asked back, putting a hint of disbelief into his own voice.

"Mariah was saying what an outdoor Eagle Scout you were. Here's your chance to impress us," Ryan said back, leaning forward aggressively.

Keitan didn't know Cotter much at all. He knew that the UVM sophomore had taken a predatory interest in Keitan's friend, Mariah Washall, and invited her and her roommate Rachel, along with Cotter's own roommate, Gary, on a hike of Mount Abraham in the Green Mountains. Mariah had in turn invited Keitan, probably because she didn't want to go without a male ally. It had sounded like a lighthearted outing, but the tension had started from the moment of introduction and escalated to disagreeable long before they summited. Now, a mile down the Long Trail, they were at the Battell shelter for the night and Ryan was upping his dominance games.

"Oh? We must have a major understanding, Ryan. I'm not here to impress you. I'm here to keep them safe," Keitan said, waving at the two girls watching worriedly. *This is it. He's gonna swing at me*, Keitan thought. The other kid was a bit taller but thinner. Keitan wasn't super worried.

Cotter's eyes widened incredulously, then he laughed. It was a real laugh, right to his core, but it wasn't a friendly laugh.

"You're—you're gonna protect them?" Cotter asked. "Who's gonna protect you, boy sprout?"

"Ryan, stop it," Mariah said, looking upset. "Keitan came so nobody would get the wrong idea. Also, he grew up around here and knows these trails."

Ryan looked at her, eyes narrowed, then glanced at Rachel. His face relaxed. "Just messin', babe," he said, then turned to look at Keitan. "Wow us, Bear Grylls."

The uneasy feeling Keitan had when Mariah first proposed the trip was now an all-stations, five-alarm bell ringing in his head. He was doubly glad he'd stopped home for an extra piece of gear from his parents' house, glad his father trusted him with the combo to the safe. Misgivings aside, he set about making a fire while the others watched.

Gathering the thin, wispy, dead limbs from the lower branches of three separate pine trees, Keitan bundled them into a twisted bird's-nest-looking bundle and set them in the fire ring. Then he spent a few minutes gathering some larger deadfall that was bone dry and easily broken into forearm-length chunks.

Last, from his cargo pants pocket, he pulled a piece of curled white birchbark he'd found on the trail and plucked his bushcraft blade from its sheath.

"That's your knife?" Ryan asked in disbelief. "That's barely a pencil sharpener."

It was actually a full four-inch blade in a drop point style, but Ryan looked like a Rambo survival knife type.

Ignoring the comment, Keitan opened the birchbark so it was flat on one of the fireplace rocks and set the edge of his knife perpendicular to the bark. Then he scraped back and forth until he had a nice little pile of bark dust and shavings. The loop on the side of his knife sheath yielded his ferrocerium fire rod and with just three scrapes of the back edge of his blade, he showered enough sparks to light the pile of shavings. Lifting the now-flaming sheet of bark, he set it under the bundle of pine twigs until the nest of mini-branches caught on its own. Flames licked up and started to hungrily consume the twigs. Layering larger and larger pieces of deadfall on the bundle created a teepee-shaped fire whose warmth brought the two girls closer, hands out.

"Now we just need to gather some bigger wood," he said, sitting back on his heels as he re-sheathed his knife and fire rod.

Ryan stood, leaning against the side of the shelter's three-walled platform, arms crossed, a frown on his face. "Correction. Now *you* gather wood. We're gonna set up the bed zone, right, Gary," he said with a sideways leer at the girls. His creepy buddy just nodded, not having said more than ten words the whole day "We've got plenty of *wood,*" Ryan said, getting a laugh from his pal.

"I'll go with you," Mariah said to Keitan.

"I'm gonna get the food going," Rachel said.

"You sure?" her roommate asked.

"Yeah, I'm fine," Rachel said, already reaching into a pack for food.

Keitan went to his own pack and disconnected the daypack portion, swinging it onto his back, with a thump. "Okay, it's getting dark. Let's gather what we can while we can still see," he said to Mariah.

They headed into the woods, immediately finding that most of the easy deadwood of the forest had already been cleaned out by waves of previous campers. They were at least three hundred yards from camp before they found a fallen spruce tree whose dead length had broken into several six and eight-foot sections.

"Perfect. Let's drag as much of this as we can," he said to Mariah.

"Keitan, I'm really sorry about this trip. Ryan was always much nicer in the dorm, but now he's acting like a real jerk."

"Which is why I'm here," he said.

"And why I'm really glad you're here. We'll get through the night and then get back tomorrow. Can we go back now? I don't like leaving Rachel alone."

He nodded, handing her the ends of two good pieces to drag, then hefted the longer, heavier bottom third of the small tree up over his own shoulder along with a four-foot section of dead birch he had found crushed under the spruce.

His day pack got snarled a bit and he had to sort it out, but no way was he going to leave it behind in camp with an asshat like Cotter. If anything, he was even more glad now of its contents.

Ryan and Gary were inside the shelter, setting out their sleeping pads and bags, and Rachel had steaks grilling on the fire and potatoes in aluminum foil in the coals. With only a one-night stay, the group had splurged on impractical but very appetizing food for their only dinner.

"Just knock the horns off mine and wipe its butt," Ryan commented from the shelter, smirking at Keitan in a nasty way.

Mariah turned toward Keitan with her back to Ryan and rolled her eyes.

Breaking up the birch, he left it near the fire, then worked on the spruce to do the same, only stacking it further from the food. Evergreens and cooking meat were not the best combination, but the birch would get them through the short amount of cooking they were gonna do.

"That smells amazing," Mariah said to her roommate.

"So do you, hot stuff!" Ryan added from thirty feet away. Kid had ears like a hawk, Keitan mused. Even buddy Gary was starting to look a bit uncomfortable with the aggressive vibe Ryan was throwing out.

"Won't these steaks draw bears?" Mariah asked.

"Very possible," Keitan said with a shrug.

"No bear will dare come anywhere near this camp," Ryan interjected, coming out of the shelter. He looked angry, like the idea was an affront to his manliness or something.

"Look, the moon's coming up," Rachel said in a completely obvious attempt at redirecting the conversation.

Somehow it worked because Ryan's head snapped around to look up at the big, yellow orb just barely visible above the eastern tree line.

"That'll help us see, right?" Mariah asked quietly, speaking to Keitan.

"Some of us can see just fine," Ryan answered her, his gaze hungry. Again, Keitan was forced to be a little impressed by the kid's hearing. He was certain that *he* couldn't have heard that if their positions had been reversed.

Ryan was looking back up at the moon and his breathing was visible. The cooling air showed clouds of breathy exhales rising over his head.

Suddenly Keitan's bad feelings coalesced into an outlandish idea, a crazy idea that he should have put out of mind instantly but the thought had already taken root in his psyche, like an invasive weed. He pulled his daypack off and turned around, walking slowly around the back of the shelter.

Once he was behind the log structure, which was like a big, three-sided lean-to, he yanked open his pack, pulled out the Hill People chest pack and snugged into it, then yanked out his packable Patagonia jacket to put over the whole thing. He felt a little better, but not fully, as his idea was still eating at his self-confidence.

He came back around the shelter only to find Ryan leaning against one wall, waiting for him.

"Cuffing the carrot, Scout? Snapping off a quick one? Maybe I'll let you watch later," he said with a wink.

"What the fuck does that mean, Ryan?" Mariah said, ten feet behind the lanky kid. Rachel stood near her, looking anxious, but Mariah just looked angry.

"What do you think it means, Cupcake? Did you think Gary and I were coming all the way out here to sing you 'Kumbaya?'" Ryan said, turning to confront her. His voice seemed deeper.

Keitan's idea was even more solid now. Ryan was a few inches taller but not any heavier, yet his mouth was writing checks that it didn't seem likely his body could back up. And he was both overly aggressive and very confident, standing with his back to an enemy who he knew had a knife. Almost like he felt invulnerable. Then there was the whole hearing thing.

Keitan patted the chest pack and its contents, then reached under his shirt for his St. Christopher's medal. The chain and medallion were both silver. Taking off the necklace, he pulled his knife from its sheath.

Ryan stiffened, tilting his head. "Pulling a blade, Scout?" he asked, voice almost a growl, but he didn't look around.

With hands that were starting to shake, Keitan held the chain over one of the back logs of the shelter and started chopping it with his knife. Adrenaline poured into his bloodstream, almost destroying his small motor control. It took two chops to get through his confirmation gift.

"What the fuck are you doing?" Ryan growled, now facing him, eyes fixed on the silver chain.

Keitan ignored him, picking up a quarter inch of silver chain with his left hand while his right dropped the knife and yanked open the back compartment of his chest pack. The grip of the Smith & Wesson 329 PD filled his hand and he yanked his dad's big woods walking revolver out. He didn't try to open the cylinder, instead just tilted the gun up and fumbled the bit of chain into the opening of the big .44 muzzle, then raised the shaking gun with both hands to cover the now wide-eyed Ryan.

"You dare?" the other boy yelled, his expression part anger and part worry. His brown eyes were clearly turning yellowish in the fading light. Then suddenly the kid was gone, just a fast dark blur running into the woods.

"What the hell? You brought a gun?" Rachel asked, shocked. "You pulled a gun on him?"

Keitan ignored her, focused on chopping the rest of the silver necklace into pieces. Pulling a speed loader of six .44 magnum hollow points from his chest pack, he started to cram the chain bits into the big hollow noses of the cartridges, wedging them into place with his knife.

"Is that silver?" Mariah asked, voice shaky.

"Yes. He's out there somewhere, Changing," Keitan said, opening the revolver's cylinder and dumping the existing rounds into his hand, then shoved them into his pants pocket. He pushed the speed loader into the empty chambers and twisted the release knob, dropping the modified rounds into place. Then he clicked the cylinder shut and moved out by the fire.

"Are you a fucking maniac? A damned gun nut?" Rachel asked. "You're fucking crazy!" She bent down to grab a stick from the piled wood and a massive dark-furred shape leapt right through the space she had just been standing in. The beast missed her completely, slamming instead into Gary, who had been standing with a shocked expression.

Keitan heard bone break and the downed boy started to yell in pain. The four-footed monster turned toward the two girls and Keitan just as Keitan pulled the trigger on the Smith and Wesson. The gun roared and the werewolf roared back in pain and anger. Giant legs contracted and sprang before Keitan could get another shot off, the werewolf disappearing into the dark.

Keitan spent ten full seconds turning in place to study the ominous dark, a small but powerful light from his pocket lighting what the bright moon didn't. Gary continued to yell and now both girls were crying, huddled together by the fire.

"We need to get him into the shelter," Keitan said. Neither girl moved. "Now!" he finally yelled, fear reducing his patience to nothing. Mariah let go of her roommate and moved to Gary, grabbing him under the arms. He proved too heavy but her sobbing friend came to her rescue, grabbing an arm and pulling harshly toward the shelter.

Gary screamed from the manhandling, then suddenly went quiet and limp, the pain finally knocking him out. The girls got him into the log shelter and Keitan backed into the space, light and gun pointed out at the night.

"Cover him with a sleeping bag. He'll be shocky when he wakes up," he said, eyes and ears on the deadly woods.

"He's a fucking werewolf?" Rachel said.

Mariah, seemingly calmer than her roommate, looked at Keitan with understanding dawning on her face. "He said he wanted to show us something this weekend. We thought he meant the view. He's been different the last few weeks. More sarcastic, quick to get angry, and really aggressive."

"Probably new to being a were," Keitan said, still watching outside. The whole world was new to werewolves, their reality, along with vampires, still a shock that society was trying to adjust to.

Something smashed the back of the shelter where the roof sloped down to its lowest point. The plywood roof split under incredible force and one massive paw was briefly visible. Rachel screamed and bolted toward the front, slamming into Keitan as he turned toward the noise. Knocked off balance, he couldn't get a shot off, instead falling onto his side, gun hand trapped by his own body. Something bigger than a paw hit the broken spot, smashing an opening that let Keitan see a massive yellow eye as he fought to get to his feet. A huge, toothy snout broke through and Keitan kicked at it with his booted foot while trying to get his gun hand out from under himself. The head snapped at his foot, biting and yanking on it before it disappeared back out of the shelter. Seconds later, there was a strike on the roof a few inches to the side of the broken hole. Keitan got to his feet, backing toward the front.

"Rachel!" Mariah yelled, running after her roommate, who was now outside the shelter. She, too, clipped Keitan, this time knocking him out the front of the open shelter. He instinctively back-rolled to his feet, still somehow holding the gun but missing the flashlight. Inside the shelter, snarls and roars sounded as the werewolf struggled to get free from the broken wood. Keitan turned and ran after the girls.

Rachel was running down the Long Trail in complete panic, Mariah behind her and Keitan last, looking over his shoulder as he went.

There was no sound but their panting breaths and pounding feet. The full moon lit the dark, muddy path just enough that they didn't fall and its silver light let Keitan see a bit of the forest around them. Behind them, a deep, cruel howl sounded through the night. They all ran faster.

Keitan thought they might have been running for three or four minutes when suddenly a voice spoke from the shadows. "Over here," a male said.

"Follow us," another voice said, this one female. Two tall strangers beckoned them and Rachel veered off the trail right to them. "We've got a camp over here. You'll be safe," the young woman said.

Mariah was now with Rachel, and Keitan had no choice but to follow, his gun down by his side. Their two saviors moved smoothly through the woods, having no issues despite the lack of a trail. Up ahead, Keitan could see the glow of firelight and in less than a minute, they were stepping out of the woods into a campsite filled with people. At least eight or maybe ten people sat or lay around a big burning fire. They looked underdressed for the woods, in jeans and t-shirts or even less. Spring in northern Vermont isn't super warm and with a clear sky overhead, the night was cold enough to see breath. Yet some of the guys were only wearing sweatpants or gym shorts and only one of the three girls he could see was wearing a coat. All eyes were on them as the group shifted around a bit and then a really, really big dude stood up. He was actually huge, not just tall but heavily built. Had to be six-six and well over two hundred and fifty pounds of muscle and black beard.

"This all of them?" the giant asked the girl.

"There's one left up at the shelter," she said. Keitan got his first good look at her in the firelight. Tall and very pretty, long brown hair and deep brown eyes. Lots of skin showing, as she was wearing just a sports bra and workout shorts. What was with these people?

"There's a werewolf up there!" he said. "We all gotta get the hell out of here."

Nobody batted an eye. "Yeah, the howl kind of gave it away," another kid said. He, at least, was wearing hiking pants and an L.L.Bean jacket. The young girl next to him was wearing almost identical clothes, and it struck him that they looked alike. "That the cannon we heard going off?" the jacket wearer asked.

Keitan started to lift his Magnum but suddenly the under-dressed brunette had his wrist in a firm grip, keeping the gun pointed at the ground. He tried to pull free but somehow she held him without even a struggle. "Easy there, buddy. Just don't want any misunderstandings, now do we?" she asked with a smile. "Oh, you're wounded?"

What? Keitan looked where she was looking and saw blood on the ankle of his right pant leg.

"It might be Ryan's. I got one shot into him," Keitan said.

"You know that even that cannon won't do much, right? Unless you're packing silver rounds," the kid in the Bean jacket said.

"Keitan chopped up his necklace and put it into his bullet things," Mariah said. "Why aren't you people freaking out? There's a real, honest-to-God, maniac werewolf out there, probably eating his roommate."

The people in the group all exchanged glances and Keitan realized they were roughly the same age as him and the girls.

"You're safe here," the giant said, his voice deep. "I'm Dellwood. That's my sister Clary. The other one who brought you in is Matthew. The outdoor gear fashionistas over there are Mack and his sister Jetta. I'll introduce the others in a bit. Right now they're gonna go look for your wolf and his friend. Go!"

It was a command and the remaining people in the group just took off into the woods like they'd been shot from a cannon.

The underdressed sister, Clary, was crouched down, inspecting Keitan's leg. "No, you got bit," she said, shaking her head and looking back at her brother.

"What? I don't even feel anything," Keitan said, kneeling down and poking at the bloody spot. A sharp pain shot up his leg. "Ow. Shit."

"Just a little one, barely bleeding," she said, watching him closely. Keitan realized she was holding his gun, somehow having taken it right out of his hand and he hadn't noticed.

"But.. but if I'm bleeding... I'm infected... right?" he asked, the truth suddenly hitting him.

"Maybe. Hard to tell," Dellwood rumbled. Clary leaned down and *sniffed* his wound. "No, you're infected," she said.

"How can you tell? I mean who can tell by sniffing... Oh shit!" Keitan said.

"What?" Mariah and Rachel asked in unison.

"They're werewolves too," he said.

"Some of us," Dellwood said, completely casual. "Others are more like werewolf hunters." His eyes turned toward the only two jacket wearers in the group.

"*Reformed* werewolf hunters," Mack said. "Ladies, please come over by the fire. You must be cold. Not everyone has the metabolism of a shrew."

Mariah looked at her roommate, then turned to Keitan. He looked at the scary Dellwood then at the really attractive girl smiling at him, holding his gun. He shrugged. "Nothing to do about it if they decide to eat us," he said, not really afraid anymore.

"Hey, hey, nobody's getting eaten around here," the girl, Jetta, said.

"Not without consent at least," Dellwood said, then laughed at his own joke.

Jetta rolled her eyes at the giant, then came forward and grabbed Rachel by the hand and Mariah by her sleeve. "Come on over here. My brother, at least, won't bite and whoever that rogue were is, he can't get past Dellwood or Clary."

"Or my sister's Glock," Mack said, rummaging in a huge cooler for bottles of water which he handed to the girls.

Keitan found himself gently guided to the fire by Clary, who gave him an encouraging smile every time he looked her way.

"Here, have a seat on the log and I'll look at your bite," the underdressed werewolf girl said.

"Why are you guys out here?" Keitan asked.

"Full moon," Mack said.

"But you and your sister aren't weres?" he asked the other boy.

"We just really like the woods," Mack said.

"But you're out here with werewolves?" Mariah asked.

"We're with them at the dorms too. Frankly I think it's much easier out here where they can Change and run after deer and stuff," Mack said. "You chopped up a necklace and made silver ammo?" he asked, turning to Keitan.

"We didn't know he was a werewolf and he got really aggressive. Basically he threatened to rape the girls," Keitan said.

"What?" Clary asked, sitting back on her heels, expression outraged.

"He's not the same kid I met in the dorm," Mariah said. "Wait... you guys live in the dorms? At UVM?"

"Separate facility downtown, but we take courses at UVM and Champlain College," Jetta said.

Suddenly, a howl rose up in the distance, followed immediately by a half dozen others, the last just outside their camp.

"They found him?" Mack asked Dellwood.

"Yeah, Curtis was the first call. The others are driving him this way," the giant said, head tilted as he listened.

"There is one... one right out there!" Rachel said, voice quivering.

"That's Matthew. He refuses to leave the area. Not really trusting the Singer kids to keep his sweetie safe," Mack said, chuckling, with a glance at his sister.

"As if I need to be kept safe," she said with a snort, smacking her brother on the arm.

"As true as that is, he can't really help himself, Jetta," Clary said. "His wolf won't let him leave you alone, especially with a rogue male on the loose."

The howls came again, closer and changing pitch through an incredible range of sounds that all made Keitan's neck hair stand up.

"Okay, they're almost here," Dellwood said, standing up. Keitan stole a look at his revolver, still in Clary's hand.

"I'd give it back, but I don't want any of our pack to get shot," she said apologetically.

"Plus, dude, it's kind of redundant with us here," Mack said, pulling a black pistol from under his coat. His sister already had a small gun in her right hand.

"Those don't look big enough," Rachel said.

"For most people, they aren't. But Mack and Jetta usually shoot things through the eye socket, so, well, no real need for a cannon," Clary said matter-of-factly.

Keitan found that really hard to believe. Through the eye? Come on. Nobody was that good of a shot.

"You said I was infected?" Keitan said to Clary, who, like her brother, was staring at the woods in the direction the howls had come from.

"Definitely," she replied.

"So I'll become a werewolf?"

She exchanged a glance with her brother. "It's a strong possibility."

"What if I chopped off my leg... below the knee?" he asked.

She turned to him, horrified.

"Wow, that's commitment!" Dellwood said. "I like this kid."

"It won't help," Clary said, flicking a glare at her brother. "It's already in your bloodstream. Already all through your body. LV is really aggressive."

Howls sounded again, so close that Mariah gasped and Rachel gave a little shriek. "Easy, girls," Mack said. "You're safe," he said, moving between them and the howls.

The two girls held hands, staring at the woods, both literally shaking, and Keitan felt like he should be doing something to help. He stood up and instantly felt a warm hand on his arm.

"Just hang easy, Keitan. We've got this. Just sit back and watch," Clary said. He was suddenly aware of her body heat, her lightly clothed body just inches from his side. He felt a wave of discomfort all over his body at the same time. Then he felt everything; the fire's heat on his back, the wind from his left, Clary's warmth on his right. He smelled the wood smoke and the woods, Clary's skin, his own blood. It suddenly sounded like a herd of elephants were crashing through the woods, headed right for them, and his vision sorta zoomed out into the forest, penetrating moon-cast shadows. Breath huffed in the night, a panting sound, and then he saw the beast, its yellow eyes spotting him as he spotted it.

It leapt, clearing twenty feet, hit the ground, already bunching up for the next leap, eyes fixed on Keitan. A dark missile hit it from the side, a furry blur as big as it was, knocking it sideways and down. The flattened werewolf was light brown, same color as Ryan's hair, the other werewolf darker. The attacking wolf had Ryan's throat in his jaws and all four legs braced as it stood over the downed wolf, growling murder.

"Submit, rogue," Dellwood said, striding up the two like they were puppies playing.

The wolf that Keitan was sure was Ryan whimpered.

"Let him up, Matt," Dellwood said, eyes on Ryan.

Matt let go and stepped back. Instantly Ryan twisted around to get his feet under him and leaped straight at Dellwood. The huge kid slapped Ryan's wolf head hard with a blurring left swing, somehow stepping sideways at the same time. Then his right hand was snaking under the wolf's throat and he was slipping around behind the wolf, climbing its back and clamping his legs around its middle.

Keitan had seen something like that in MMA fights, but never between a huge man and a giant beast.

Massive arms tightened around the thick, furred throat as even bigger legs scissored the werewolf's middle.

"And it's Singer with the rear naked choke," Mack narrated, like it was Monday Night Fights.

Cabled arms flexed, barely moving as the wolf went apeshit. Something like ten or twenty seconds went by and the wolf's struggles slowed. Keitan became aware that massive wolves were all around them and that the wolf that had pinned Ryan first was now just on Clary's other side. Just in front of Jetta, who watched the fight like she might be tested on it, one hand on her hip and the other hanging by her side, pistol pointed at the ground.

The wolf that was Ryan slumped, eyes closed and the body relaxed. Dellwood released it and untangled himself from it, climbing easily back to his feet.

"You have to hold the choke a lot longer with weres," he said, directing his words right at Keitan. "So you have to be sure if it's a were or a human. Choke a human that long and he may die. Got it?"

Confused at the seeming lesson, Keitan just nodded. Sure. Anything you say, Mister Chokes
Werewolves With His Bare Hands.

"Don't worry. We practice this stuff all the time. We'll get you up to speed," Dellwood said.

"Ah Dell, give him a break; he just got bit. Let him process," Clary said, shifting even closer till her too-hot skin was actually pressed against Keitan.

Dellwood eyed his sister's movements, raising one eyebrow, then grinning. "Just facing the inevitable, little sis."

On the ground, Ryan's paws twitched.

"Let's truss him up," Dellwood said, looking back down. A muscular naked guy stepped out of the woods to the left and walked unconcerned to a pack, bending down to dig through it. The guy tossed a loop of wire at Dellwood, then pulled gym shorts from the bag, which he proceeded to pull on.

Suddenly there were a whole bunch of naked guys and one naked girl, all nonchalantly pulling on pants or shorts. Keitan didn't know where to look. It seemed like a real, real bad idea to offend anyone who could turn into a massive killing machine. He felt eyes on him and turned to see Clary smiling at him.

"We aren't modest," she said. "You'll get used to it."

"What's going to happen to him?" Mariah asked, staring at the unconscious wolf.

"We're gonna take him to the local pack Alpha," Dellwood said. "This really isn't our territory although he lets us run around in it. We're all transplants going to school."

"What will he do?" Mariah pressed.

"Either straighten his shit out or put him down. Frankly, engineering a trip to rape the two of you doesn't speak well for his future. We don't put up with that shit," Dellwood said.

"He'll also want to know how the kid got bit. Hey, how's the other one?"

Another naked guy walked out of the woods, Gary hanging limp over his shoulder like a rolled-up beach towel. "Broken leg. Keeps passing out."

"Put him over here, Brian. We'll splint that leg," Jetta said, rummaging in a pack and pulling out a first aid kit. Keitan noticed the gun had disappeared.

Brian set the unconscious kid down, not quite dropping him but non-too gentle, then sauntering over to grab some clothes, deliberately passing close by Rachel and Mariah, who didn't seem to know where to look.

Keitan moved over to watch Mack and Jetta prepare a splint for Gary's leg, both working with an efficiency that he admired.

"You really chopped up your necklace?" Mack asked.

"Only silver I had," Keitan said, reaching into his pocket for the last piece. His finger suddenly stung and he yanked it out like a hornet was in his pocket.

"You'll need to be careful around silver now," Clary said, suddenly at his side. She offered him his revolver and he quickly pulled his finger from his mouth to put the gun away.

"That's a good sign, right?" Mack asked Clary, pointing at Keitan's finger.

"A very good sign," she said, with a smile for Keitan. She turned and walked over to her brother. Keitan found himself admiring the view as she did.

"Why is it good?" he asked absently.

"Because the alternative is bad," Mack said cheerily.

"What?" Keitan asked, but Clary was suddenly by his side.

"Come on, let's go pack up your camp," she said.

"Now? In the dark?"

Her brows rose just slightly and she tilted her head, lips in a flat line.

"Oh, right. Nothing to worry about. The werewolves are on my side," he said.

She smiled and grabbed his hand, pulling him inexorably toward the trail. Right, best go with the girl who can pluck your arms from their sockets without breaking a sweat, he thought, yet somehow, in some half-crazy way, he wasn't afraid.

Forty minutes later, they were back. Keitan noticed that Rachel and Mariah were asleep, curled up together on a blanket next to the fire. A few of the wolves, about five, were missing, as were Gary and Ryan, who had been trussed up with silvery cable when Keitan left.

"You got grease on your mouth, champ," Mack said to Keitan, who instantly rubbed the back of his hand across his face.

"Smells like steak," Matthew said from twenty feet away. "Burnt steak."

"They left the food when they ran. He got really hungry when he smelled it," Clary said, with a huge smile, like he wasn't a burnt steak hog but had done something really good. "Gave me some of it too," she added, looking down at the pile of gear she was making on the ground, a little smile on her face.

Across the clearing, Dellwood spun around, eyes wide, mouth dropping open. "And *you* ate it?" he asked, incredulous.

"Is that surprising? Don't you like steak?" Keitan asked, totally confused.

"Steak is great," she said, not looking up as she put a sleeping pad on the top of the pile. Then she moved over to the fire and helped herself to a bottle of water from the cooler, throwing Keitan a second bottle.

He wasn't expecting it, but somehow snatched it out of the air. "Thanks," he said, eyes on the massive Dellwood, who was approaching like an avalanche. The giant stopped in front of the smaller male, studying him as if he was just seeing him. Then he glanced back at his sister, who was watching with narrowed eyes. Then, he... shrugged.

"Okay then. I'll be keeping my eye on you... Keitan was it?" Dellwood said before turning and walking away.

"What does that mean?" Keitan asked Mack as he settled on a log in a spot that just happened to be right next to Clary. Jetta was exchanging grins with Clary but Mack stayed focused on him.

"It means welcome to the Pack. Your life just changed," Mack said, leaning back and propping his feet up on a log. He shivered, zipping up his jacket.

Keitan realized he wasn't wearing his, just wearing a t-shirt. But he wasn't cold. At all. Realization hit him and he turned to look next to him. Deep brown eyes met his and she gave him a nod and a smile.

Holy shit, life had changed, and finals weren't even here yet.

Boredom killed the Vampire

Oddly, when people live long past their expiration dates, centuries beyond normal lifespans, one of the biggest dangers is almost the same thing that they have to survive to get through their teen years—boredom.

The little bar in Western Pennsylvania normally had much quieter Tuesday nights. It mostly just broke even for the overhead of having a single bartender and one waitress on duty, sometimes not even doing that.

But this night was different. The four or five regulars had made phone calls when the celebrities showed up, bringing in ten times more customers, all eager to see the fun.

"We didn't have to do this," the tall, lanky kid said to his platinum-blonde girlfriend.

"Listen punk, you only turn twenty-one once," a spiky-haired slip of a brunette answered instead.

"But I don't even drink, Lydia," the youth said, watching his girlfriend toss down a shot of Jack Daniels that had appeared unbidden in front of her. People, mostly men but a few women too, all over the bar were sending drinks to the famous group of heroes who had come to town for a demonic monster but were now just celebrating a birthday. Well, sending them mostly to Stacia.

"Not the point. It's the fact that you're legal, at least to be in a dive like this, that counts. Good thing you're already legal for other things or blondie here would be in jail," the little vampire said.

"Yeah, like a jail could actually keep me," Stacia said with a snort. "Hey, that's *Heart* playing—*Magic Man.* Come on, Declan. We're dancing."

She grabbed his hand and towed him to the tiny dance floor, spinning into a lithe dance move that did nothing to cool the ardor of her many fans around the pub.

To his credit, the tall kid went with the flow of it, dancing to the best of his admittedly low ability, knowing that no one was going to be watching *him* anyway.

Across the room, seated on the far side of the bar, three men in various states of inebriation watched the gorgeous blonde dancing with her gawky partner.

"She's way, way, way too hot for that little shit," one of the said.

"Like she'd ever go for you, Dave," his friend laughed.

"I'm way more man that that little kid," Dave said, slurring a couple of words.

"Dude, you forgetting what she is?" the third friend said. He was the least drunk of the three, and his expression was wary as he too watched the lithesome figure dance fifty feet away. He drained his beer and stood up. "I gotta drain the dragon. Don't you idiots get into trouble while I'm gone."

"Fuck you," Dave said, but his tone was mild and without malice. His eyes were still locked on the famous figure he had previously only seen on the Internet, in magazines, and on television.

The soberest one snorted and headed to the men's room.

"I bet she'd forget about him quick if she got a load of me," Dave said.

"You mean a load *from* you," the second said, laughing at his own joke.

"Skinny kid is punk," a new, deeper voice said from behind them. Both men turned and looked back, then up, and then up again. A massive figure stood there, the biggest man either had ever seen in person. He was mean looking, heavily muscled, and scary as hell.

"Ah, what?" the second one asked.

"I am in agreement. Skinny kid is punk. You should punch him in face," the huge man said with a heavy Russian accent. He held a beer pitcher in one hand and was drinking from it like it was a mug. In his huge fist, it actually looked like that's what it was.

"Oh, we were just talking shit. You know? Like she could do better," the second one said with an uncertain glance at his buddy.

"You are right," the giant said. "You are much better for her than skinny punk. Go punch in face," the giant said, clapping Dave on his shoulder and almost collapsing him off the chair.

Bringing himself back upright, he looked shocked but then nodded. "I am, aren't I?"

"Much. You are much more man than little boy trying to dance," the giant said with a nod toward the couple on the dance floor.

"He's got no moves," Dave said.

“I don’t know, Dave. She seems pretty into him,” the second said.

“Bah. Because she has not seen you—Dave,” the giant said, smiling. It was as if he was attempting reassurance, but it missed the mark. Both men were unsettled but looking back at the lithesome girl on the dance floor, Dave came to a decision. He stood up, wobbled a bit, and headed for the dance floor. His partner hesitated, then quickly slid down from his own stool and followed.

They were almost to the small open space when a hand clamped down on Dave’s shoulder. He spun around and found himself face-to-face with his third buddy, newly back from the men’s room.

“What are you idiots doing?”

“I’m going to punch that punk in the face and introduce myself to *her*,” Joe said, weaving a bit as he pointed at the platinum blonde.

“Whoa, whoa, where did that stupid idea come from?” the third guy asked.

“The giant,” Dave said. His partner nodded and turned to point behind them. The only guy in sight was an old man at the bar who likely topped out at five-six or five-seven. Dave and his buddy looked at each other and shrugged, then turned back to their smarter pal.

“No, no, no. She’s the white werewolf, right?” the sober one asked. They both nodded. “She’s supposed to go out with the dude the papers call the Warlock, right?” They nodded again. “She’s dirty dancing with that guy like he’s her boyfriend, right?” Both wobbly heads swiveled to look at the dancers, then came back to him. "I guess," Dave admitted. His other buddy nodded.

"So. Did you maybe think that the skinny kid is the Warlock?" Mr. Logical asked.

"Ah, what?" Dave asked. Three seconds later, the math worked itself out in his head. "Oh."

His partner in crime was already staring at the skinny dancer, his eyes wide.

"So, if he is the Warlock, what do you geniuses think will happen if you try to punch him in the face?"

"He'll curse me and my dick will fall off?" Dave asked.

"If you're lucky. Come on you two, let's get away from temptation," the smart one said, leading his drunk buddies away.

From the opposite side of the bar, deep in the shadows, Arkady, Chief of Demidova Security, sighed to himself. So close. Oh well, adapt and carry on, he thought. New plan.

Ghosting by the locals, moving in almost utter silence, he approached the bar, looming over it and getting the immediate attention of the bartender. "Four fingers of rum," he said, tossing a fifty-dollar bill onto the bar top. Seconds later, he carried his rock glass, brimming with Bacardi, back around to the table claimed by his team. Lydia was out on the dance floor with Declan and Stacia, leaving the table empty. Chris and Tanya were back at the hotel with the twins, relaxing after the demonic exorcism that Chris had performed three hours earlier. Nika was out on a solo mission or he wouldn't have even tried any of this.

Settling into the sturdiest of the chairs, he watched the dancers carefully. Timing was everything. At the appropriate moment, when both girls were turned away and Declan was watching Stacia, he dumped the glass of rum into the single pitcher of cola on the table. Then he leaned back and waited.

Two songs later, Declan headed back to the table and collapsed into a chair. He gave the giant vampire security chief a nod and drained off the soda already in his glass. Then he refilled the glass from the plastic pitcher. Arkady smiled at him and raised his own beer pitcher in salute. Declan raised his glass and leaned forward to sip it but suddenly had a lap full of blonde.

"Tired already?" Stacia asked with a smirk.

"Dehydrated. Plus it's fun to watch," he said with a grin.

"Oh, that's how it is, is it? Oh wait, that's Warren Zevon. 'Werewolves of London,'" his girlfriend said, hopping smoothly off his lap and dragging him back to the dance floor, soda still in hand. Lydia, coming off the dance floor, snagged his drink and took a sip as she headed for the table.

Then she froze, her head coming up to look at the soda. Her eyes swiveled to the pitcher of cola, which she snagged in a blur. Sniffing its contents, she turned and leveled her green eyes on Arkady. "Tell me he didn't drink any of that?"

"Boy is twenty-one. Legal to drink."

"Boy is the most dangerous witch on the planet whose thoughts become reality. What damage could a drunk superwitch do?" she asked.

"That would be fun to see," the giant said, not meeting her eyes.

"Fun? Arkady, how fun would it be if he decided to wonder whether your vampire insides looked like a regular human's? Regular witches have to chant or sing or say spells in special ways to get magic to work. He thinks about it and it happens. He doesn't drink because he's terrified of what he might do drunk. You think this was a good idea?"

"You are baby. Have not seen even one full century," he said, dismissing her comments.

"Oh, that's what this is? Mister alive-for-centuries is bored? And you thought you'd mess with the birthday boy? The one we all worry will go off the deep end? How will your queen feel about that?"

"You squeal to her like snitch?" he asked, his full attention now locked on the tiny vampire.

"About most stuff? Never. About things that effect the mental security of Harry freaking-super Potter out there? You betcha. Senka too. This is really serious, Arkady."

"If he is so unstable that a drop of rum is doomsday, maybe he should be ended?" Arkady said.

Out on the dance floor, Stacia suddenly stopped dancing and spun around to stare at Arkady. Her eyes had gone completely yellow.

"Are you a complete moron? Oh, still trying to *liven* things up? Omega, please inform Tanya that her Chief of Security is precipitating an incident with the witch and the wolf," Lydia said.

"Bah! You have no honor," Arkady said, hissing at the smallest vampire in the Coven.

She didn't bat an eye. "No, what I have is duty!" she said. "And unlike you, I do it."

The giant pulled back as if slapped. Then he turned to look at the young couple on the dance floor. Stacia looked ready to fight and Declan, who was looking around, confused, was making the bar's lights flicker as he prepared for whatever had alarmed his girl.

There was a sharp snapping sound and Arkady vanished from sight, the pub's door slamming open by itself.

Stacia moved over to Lydia, her young witch boyfriend following with a bewildered look on his face.

"What was that?" Stacia demanded.

"That was boredom," Lydia said, looking worried. "It's the number one killer of old Darkkin."

"What happened?" Declan asked. "Arkady is... bored?"

"Living for hundreds of years is not as easy as it sounds. Year after year of doing the same thing wears away at the psyche. You ever wonder why there aren't any Darkkin older than Senka?" Lydia asked.

"I try not to think about Senka at all," the young witch said. "She scares me spitless."

Lydia looked at him like she was trying to decide if he was joking. Then she snorted. "Anyone ever tell you you're one of a kind, kid?"

"Mostly they just want to know *what* kind I am," he said. "What did he do?"

"He tried to stir up trouble," Lydia said. "What might be mostly minor stuff in most situations but maybe rather more drastic in this one."

Declan frowned before turning to Stacia to see if she was following the little vampire's cryptic words.

"He spiked your Coke with rum," the blonde werewolf said.

"I would have tasted it and spit it out," Declan said with a shrug.

"Would you?" Lydia asked, unconvinced.

"Of course. I know what rum tastes like. I've tasted gin, vodka, whiskey, scotch, tequila," he said, shuddering at the last one, "and a bunch of other stuff. Just so I knew what they tasted like."

"But you just turned twenty-one today?" Lydia asked.

"Aunt Ash had me taste all the bar stuff at Rowan West a long time ago. Said we needed to do away with the mystery. She even let me get a little drunk once. Put me in a circle and blocked my access to magic. It was really scary. The room spun, I couldn't think straight, and I had the worst headache the next day."

"And you never wanted to taste it again?" Lydia asked, looking at him like he was an alien.

"I don't think you realize how important control is to a witch. None of the witches at Arcane drink."

"Oh," Lydia said, expression changing to reflective. She tapped her bottom lip for a second. "It's possible, I suppose, that I may have overreacted."

"What did you think? That I would drink a rum and Coke without tasting it and get blotto? Oh? You did," he said, face flooding with realization. "You thought I'd lose control and like go crazy or something."

He sat down in a chair looking stunned. Lydia looked at Stacia, a really worried look on her face. Stacia was frowning at the little vampire, but turned her attention to her boyfriend.

"Would you be worried?" she asked him.

"What?"

"Would *you* be worried if a witch with your power got drunk?" Stacia asked him.

He frowned and opened his mouth to protest but stopped and closed it. "Wow, there should be smoke or something," Lydia said, looking at him closely, then raised a quick hand in apology. "Sorry, can't stop the snark sometimes."

"I get your point, but I would know that the witch in question wouldn't get drunk," he said.

"Nah, let's say he or she got drugged. Some tasteless Rufilin or something," Stacia pressed.

"I would wrap her up in a circle till she sobered up," he said.

"What if she was too powerful to circle? Or maybe I should ask if your witch pack would be able to contain you if you got drugged?" Stacia asked.

"Oh. Yeah," he said, face going pale. "Point."

"But I overreacted," Lydia said.

"One, Arkady shouldn't be trying shit like that with a teammate, and two, you didn't know Declan was prepared for something like rum," Stacia said. "New procedure," she said, turning to Declan. "You don't ever drink anything that you don't prepare or see get prepared or, if in question, have me sniff."

"I will analyze all of your drinks ahead of time, Father," Omega said from Lydia's phone, which sat on the tabletop.

"So why did Arkady take off?" Stacia asked.

"I, may have, hit him a bit below the belt," Lydia said.

Declan looked shocked for a second, then grunted. "Figuratively, I'm guessing."

"Of course, numbskull. I may have implied that he wasn't fulfilling his duty... to Tanya."

"Ouch," Stacia said. Declan was nodding, eyes wide. "What should we do?" he asked.

"You? Nothing. Me? I need to go find him, if I can," Lydia said, looking uncertain.

Declan coughed.

"What? You know where he is?" she asked, clearly in disbelief.

"Me? No. Omega, on the other hand..." he trailed off.

"He's got drones on Arkady?" Lydia asked.

"No, but he can likely predict where he'll be," Declan said.

"There is a ninety-three percent chance that Arkady is patrolling a perimeter around the hotel where Tanya, Chris, and the twins are," Omega said.

"That makes sense. I kick him in his honor and duty and he heads out to make sure the queen is safe," Lydia said. "Omega, you scare me sometimes. Mostly late in the day when I'm supposed to be sleeping. The rest of the time, I'm too busy thanking the Universe for you."

"As you say, Lydia, predicting Arkady's whereabouts is something you likely would have come up with, given time."

"Yeah. Right. That's it exactly," the little vampire said, rolling her eyes. "You two stay here. I'm gonna find the big guy and have a chat."

The witch and the wolf glanced at each and then looked back at her. "Nah, we're done here. Getting a bit crowded."

Fifteen minutes later, Lydia parked the rental car in the hotel lot. "You really think he's out there?" she asked the other two as they all got out of the car.

Declan squatted down and put his hand against the pavement of the parking lot. His eyes lost focus for a few seconds, then he nodded. He pointed diagonally at the building. "He's on the other side of the hotel. Standing motionless."

"Okay, that's creepy. What, did the earthworms tell you that?" Lydia asked, glancing at Stacia, who just shrugged.

"It's kinda like what happens on Fairie, just severely limited in distance. Maybe a quarter mile or so," the young warlock answered.

"And you've been able to do this how long?"

"Well, after we got back from Fairie, I sorta experimented a bit. No biggie," he said.

"Un-huh. Right. Well, you lovebirds head on in. I've got some chatting to do."

"Lydia, I don't think Declan is mad or anything but I am. Messing around like that could have gotten civilians hurt, damaged our goodwill, and any number of things," Stacia said.

"Yes. I know. That's why, while I have to make an apology, I also have to remind him of all that."

She found him pretty close to where Declan had pointed, at the far corner of the hotel. He was standing, facing away from the hotel, which happened to be east.

"Waiting for the rising sun?" she asked.

He grunted, just slightly.

"So the kid says he would have tasted the rum and spit it out. I might have overreacted. I'm sorry about that," she said.

"Not so much," he said, still facing away.

"Nah, the kid's tried a bunch of alcohol already. His aunt even let him get drunk once to show him how bad it was for him," Lydia said.

"I did not know," he said.

"Yeah, so no big deal."

"No. I did not know," he said, turning to her at last. "I thought he would drink and get drunk."

"Oh. And you actually *wanted* a drunk super witch?" she asked.

He turned back to the eastern sky, which was still the deep dark of full night. After a second, he spoke.

"Dah. Seemed like fun," he said.

"Really? Because it doesn't seem like fun to me. Hey, you helped train the kid, right? You don't think a drunk Declan would be an issue?"

"Always held back," he said.

"You always held back?"

"No. Skinny witch always held back. Never let go."

"I always heard from Tanya and Chris that once you guys got him started, he was kind of a lot to handle?" she asked.

"Dah," he said. "Always wanted to see him let go a bit. *That* would be something to see."

"Yeah, up until he dropped a building on you, burned you up in a fire tornado, or just flat out made the ground open up and swallow everything," she said.

He turned and met her eyes. After a second, he nodded. "Dah," he said, turning away.

"Is it really that bad?" she asked. "I mean you've got demon-hunting rookie cops, teenaged warlocks, werewolves everywhere, twin vampire babies, a world-dominating super computer, and alien enemies out the ass. Oh, and a beautiful telepath who can read you like a book. What more could you want?"

"Not bored with life, just bored right now," he said with a shrug.

"And that's worth winding the kid up and letting him spin through a whole town?"

"No. Was mistake."

"Oh. So you're standing guard against the sun for what? Penance?"

"Am considering resignation," he said.

"What? Because you tried to get the kid drunk?"

"Also tried to get men to punch him."

"Wow, something about the kid really bothers you, huh?"

"Nah. Just easy target. Men get stupid looking at the wolf girl," he said.

"You can use her name—Stacia. And yes, stupid men are everywhere. That one would have been even less of an issue. Have you ever seen her deal with drunk assholes? Hilarious. *That* would have been entertaining. Hell, I might help you next time," she said.

"No next time. Bad judgement. Might have ruined all of my queen's plans," he said.

"Admittedly not your best idea, but *I* get to be the judge of your employability," Tanya said suddenly from out of the darkness. Both of them whirled around, finding their young boss standing only twenty feet away, blue eyes almost glowing.

"My queen," Arkady said, instantly dropping to one knee, head bowed.

"I am," she said with a nod. "Which means you must abide by *my* will, yes?"

He looked up at her, trapped. After several long seconds, he nodded.

"And my will is that you will continue to be my Chief of Security until such time as I say otherwise," Tanya said. "Also, no more trying to slip anything into Declan's drinks or food, right?"

He nodded again.

"I do kinda like the idea of messing with *her* with drunk guys, though," Tanya said.

"Was messing with boy witch," he said, frowning.

"Same thing," she said, waving off the difference.

"Hah," Lydia said. "You're just pissed because humans find *her* more approachable than you."

"I don't want a bunch of drunk, smelly humans approaching me," Tanya said with a sniff.

"Probably not, but it bothers you just the same," Lydia said, wagging a finger.

"She turns into a hulking, slobbering monster. How can they forget that?" Tanya said.

"First, she isn't married to God's Hammer. Kind of a disincentive to hitting on you. Second, men are extremely visual, as you already know. Combine that with alcohol and you get—presto—horny idiots," Lydia said.

"She does have a super witch, though," Tanya pointed out, not willing to concede the argument.

Lydia sighed. "A) there aren't many photos that survive his vigilant offspring's attention, so nobody really knows him on sight, and B) he looks like a dorky kid still. Acts like it too. You should have seen him dancing. Hardly a threatening sight."

Tanya smiled. "That *would* be funny to see. I suppose wolf girl dances just fine?"

"Yeah, she's like sex in motion. We should all dance together at Plasma. That would fire up the masses," Lydia said.

"Always the peace councilor, aren't you, Chapman?" Tanya asked.

"Her wolf is besotted with the kid and by now, so is she. He can literally move the earth for her, plus he's got his own foreign nation on another frigging planet. She doesn't want your man," Lydia said.

Tanya looked at Lydia for a moment or two, considering. "What do you think, Chief of Security?"

"Girl keeps creepy warlock kid in line. Full-time job," he said.

"Really? A five-hundred-year-old vampire warrior calling a twenty-one-year-old Irish boy creepy?" Lydia asked.

"Dah. Spooky too," the giant said, face completely serious.

"You two done? I've got teething babies to deal with," Tanya said.

"Bah. Auntie Lydia is here. I'll just let them chew on old leathery Russian vampires."

"Oh yeah? Then guess what? You've got a deal. Night's still young. I'm going out with my guy," Tanya said.

Arkady raised his hand and pushed a button on his computer watch. "Klaus, get the car ready for the young queen. She and her Chosen are going out."

"*Roger that,*" came the response.

"And you?" Tanya asked.

"Have babies to guard," he said.

She nodded. "Good. Because the number of people I trust to protect my kids can be counted on one hand and most of them are right here."

"Dah," he said with a twitch of his lips that might, just might, have been a smile.

Author's post notes:

The second volume of the Compendium will follow *very* quickly, and will feature another batch of your favorite characters filling in the gaps, so to speak. In addition, please page forward to read the first two chapters of a new sci-fi series I'm launching, the Zone War series. This is a straight science fiction story but I think most readers of the Demon Accords will like this series as well. The Demon Accords will, of course, continue on with the next full book coming right after Accords Compendium, Volume 2.

Zone War

By John Conroe

Chapter 1

"And now for today's addition of Zone War. *Viewers are warned that this presentation may include sudden images of extreme graphic violence, including death. This production is unscripted and carried live in unedited format for an authentic viewing experience. Under no circumstances should any viewer attempt to enter the Manhattan Drone Zone without explicit authorization by the Department of Defense Zone Exclusion Authority. All of the salvage and bounty personnel depicted are duly licensed and trained professionals. There are no amateurs in* Zone War, *and Flottercot Productions is not liable for any injuries or deaths incurred by viewers of this program."*

Of course I had to cross the living room at that exact moment, my bowl of ice cream balanced on my work tablet. I had timed my foray into the kitchen with exacting precision, determined to be in and out in under two minutes, which was the amount of time till that blasted show started. The rest of my family was huddled around the viewing wall in anticipation of the daily showing of what was currently the most popular reality show in the world. Not being able to find the ice cream scoop had foiled my plan.

The screen melted from a black background with floating words to a live feed showing bouncing footage of one of downtown Manhattan's deserted streets, husks of cars littered about. The sun was out and the camera mounted on the outside of the LAV was broadcasting a clear, high def picture, even if it was shaky from the vehicle's ride.

Catching the opening scene was my first piece of bad luck. The second was Monique catching sight of me in the corner of her eye. "Hey, AJ's here. You gonna watch it with us this time? Or hide in your room?"

"I'm going to *work* in my room, little sister, so that *we* can get paid for what *I* brought out yesterday," I said.

The little sister part was ill-advised on my part, as it was guaranteed to trigger her twin's temper. Gabby whipped around on the couch and glared at me. "Oh, is *big* brother busy saving the day?"

Fourteen-year-old girls should come with the same kind of hazard warning labels used for explosives and poisons. I'd rather face the Zone any day than get drawn into a verbal war with my lethal little sisters, who fire off words faster than a Russian Wolf anti-personnel drone fires flechettes.

"Gabby, enough. Ajaya's work is important to this family and you know it. All of our BUIs together aren't enough to support us, even with your father's death benefit," my mother said, shutting down the more volatile of the twins. Then she turned my way. "And you, Ajaya Edward Gurung, how many times have I warned you about arrogance?"

"I wasn't being arrogant, Mom. I was making the point that I have other things to do besides watch that crap, especially when I can see it in person any day I want—if I want to take the risk of being near them," I said, moderating my tone.

Behind my mother, the terrible twins both raised their hands and enacted individual ceremonial displays of the middle finger. Monique chose to pull off the imaginary top of her middle finger lipstick and apply a liberal dose to her lips, while Gabrielle blew into her thumb to inflate her own middle digit.

My eyes flicked their way and then back to my mother, whose face had taken on her stoic look. The one where she tries not to crumble for fear of my weekly forays into what was regularly described by the Zone War narrator as the most dangerous place on Earth.

And it was. Take the island of Manhattan, release over twenty-five thousand highly advanced Russian, Chinese, and Indian autonomous war drones in a single stunning act of terrorism, and let simmer for ten years. The result was the one borough of New York City that was completely devoid of human inhabitants and whose artificially intelligent denizens aggressively kept it that way.

It was estimated that over three hundred and seventy-two thousand people lost their lives in the first week of the Manhattan Attack. Another twenty-three thousand died during the second week, as rescue operations and military units counterattacked. Only a crazy fast response by US special operations ready reaction teams, in coordination with New York National Guard, FBI, NYPD, and a whole alphabet of other federal groups, kept the drones from escaping into the other four boroughs. The whole world almost died as an enraged America brought the doomsday clock to eleven-fifty-nine and fifty-nine seconds, saved by uncharacteristic transparency on the part of Russia, India, and China, who all stepped up to provide assistance and data about their drone weapon systems and particularly against the terrorists.

Ten years later, the terrorists who were responsible, the Gaia Group, were completely obliterated, hunted with a chilling ruthlessness by a fiercely unified United States. The borough island, however, was still a no man's land. And a rich one at that.

Everyone in Manhattan either fled or died in not much more than a few days' time. One of the wealthiest communities on Earth became empty so fast that countless riches, both literal and information-based, were left lying around for anyone to pick up. Anyone who could get safely past the lethal new owners, that is. Hence *Zone War*, a show that followed five salvage teams as they braved the Zone on a regular basis to pull out abandoned riches and kill drones. The Zone was also the source of my income, the money that kept my family afloat after Wall Street crashed, was abandoned, then relocated piecemeal to backup sites around the East Coast. The massive worldwide recession that followed dwarfed all others before it. Ten years later, the world economy was just now starting to see the sprouts of fiscal recovery. Yes, we all received the Basic Universal Income checks that were paid out to all Americans, but that wasn't enough to do more than cover bare necessities, as Mom had said.

Zone War was a huge success, a show that followed the flashiest and noisiest salvage teams. And none of them made more noise than Johnson Recovery.

"Oh, Ajaya, there is your girl," Aama said from her spot between my sisters. My father's mother is quite the romantic. Both of my sisters turned and gave me their best smirks. I ignored them, but I couldn't quite bring myself to ignore the monitor. Onscreen, the camera had switched to the face of the LAV driver. The blonde, blue-eyed Scandinavian goddess of the drone hunt, Astrid Johnson.

The youngest member of Johnson Recovery, a.k.a. Team Johnson, Astrid was the principal LAV driver but also filled the role of overwatch sharpshooter when more than two of the team deployed from their armored vehicle. A beautiful, smart, and very tough girl, she was hugely popular across the nation and probably most of the globe, a role model for girls and an object of fantasy for guys of all ages. I've known her since we were both ten.

Only her oldest brother, JJ, was as popular. Tall, muscular, and bold, JJ was the JR point man for ground deployments, and his media nickname was Thor, possibly because of the big sledgehammer he used to break into buildings, possibly because of his blond good looks. Women sure seemed to dig him.

You had to give him his due. Even with full body armor, he took enormous risk every time he stepped foot on Manhattan soil, mostly due to his father's preferred approach to things—drive fast and loud, shoot everything in sight, and then haul ass back out at extreme speed. Right on cue, the camera view switched to show JJ standing with his father, Brad, just behind the driver's seat.

Brad Johnson, or Colonel Brad Johnson, was ex-US Army. He'd started his career in tanks, then moved into a Stryker Brigade Combat Team, and never looked back. He and the rest of his family were in Manhattan, visiting an old military friend, on the night the drones were released. They escaped, as did their host family. Drone Night was a life-changing event for anyone who survived it and Brad Johnson was as affected as anyone—maybe more so. Within a year, Brad had quit the military and the Johnsons had relocated to Brooklyn. Brad started Zone salvage work, even as the military was still permanently blockading the island. He started work with his military friend, an ex-British SAS sniper named Baburam Gurung—my father. Eventually they had a falling out over work methods and went their separate ways.

I turned away from the show and walked out of the room, down the hall, and into my bedroom, which is also my office. Time to make some money.

Chapter 2

"Status?" I asked.

"Current bids on items one through ten, twelve, and fourteen are all below reserve level," my personal AI reported. *"Items eleven, thirteen, and fifteen have been purchased for the Buy Now price."*

"Time left on remaining items?"

"Fourteen hours and seven minutes."

There are almost as many ways to make money in the Zone as there are ways to die. Almost. The most common is salvage. The New York State court system ruled that anything found and recovered inside the exclusion zone was the property of the finder. Manhattan was chock full of stuff to find: from cash, gems, jewelry, art, furniture, fashion items, and electronics, to corporate secrets and proprietary information on stand-alone computer systems abandoned in the attack.

The Johnson family had proven to be experts at monetizing the Zone. Initially, Brad and my father had brought out cash that they recovered from stores and banks. Nowadays, the JR team just went in hell bent for leather, raided an art gallery, jeweler's, or even an haute fashion store, and bulled their way back out. Only licensed recovery agents were allowed onto the island, but the Johnsons also acted as guides, highly paid ones, for rich people who wanted to experience shooting a Chinese Raptor drone or firing a .50 caliber anti-material rifle into a Tiger drone. Then there were the massive studio fees paid to the on-air talent that made *Zone War* the top show on the globe. Yes, the other teams contributed to the popularity, but the attractive Scandinavian war family was top draw. If you don't believe me, just count the ads you see some or all of them in. Hocking everything from the latest workout clothes to Astrid's own line of makeup for combat to JJ's signature basketball shoes.

As wealthy as they had become, the JR Team's approach to salvage left a lot to be desired, especially if you wanted a really tricky recovery, like say corporate intellectual property left on the twenty-second floor of a downtown high rise. Their bull-in-a-china shop approach stirred up every drone in a half mile radius, leaving them with just a handful of minutes to extract their valuables before the sheer numbers would overwhelm even their heavily armored vehicles.

That's where I came in. Gurung Extraction had a sterling reputation for bringing back hard-to-recover items. That's because I'm stealthy AF. Slip in and slip out. Part training by my sniper dad and part tech magic of my own design. The things I was selling on the Zone-ite auction site were just extra, mostly jewelry, that I found along my way. We also had a pretty good family bank account going, the result of stashing any and all cash picked up during my Zone travels. That was going to pay the twins' way through college. But the real money came from specific recovery missions.

"You have three new queries for services."

"Summarize, please." For some reason, I was always polite with AI. Most people weren't. It just seemed right somehow.

"One is a request for choice items of sports memorabilia housed in a private collection in the Upper West Side, the second for recovery of legal papers from a personal residence, and the third is a corporate query for proprietary software in a Wall Street trading office."

"Triage, please."

"The corporate request is the only one that meets or exceeds your risk-reward minimum offer. The sports request is not remotely rewarding enough, and the stated offer for the legal papers is far below the corporate query. Additionally, there is a time-adjusted bonus for the recovery of the computer records."

"Display."

The one blank wall in my room lit up with the email including two financial numbers, the main offer and the bonus, each of which were large enough to make me set my ice cream aside. Somebody really wanted their algorithms. Which immediately begged the question as to why now—ten years later? Actually reading the email all the way through answered that question, or at least provided *an* answer.

"—Zone recovery rates of success have not been deemed sufficient until now to attempt salvage," I read out loud. "Somebody's been paying attention to Gurung Extraction," I mused. The corporate name on the email was something called the Zeus Global Finance Corporation.

"Correct. ISP addresses assigned to Zeus Global Finance began viewing the Gurung Extraction website two weeks ago. Additional bot searches on the web have left sufficient evidence to indicate a relatively deep review of Arya assignments to date."

I thought about the offer, then reread the few details of the extraction that were listed.

"Did Zeus Global have an office on Wall Street?"

"Negative. However, the Zeus website lists two corporate executive officers who were employed by a different firm, now defunct, that did have offices near Wall Street ten years ago."

The wall view changed to list the two officers as the Chief Investment Officer and Chief Financial Officer, complete with pictures, as well as a side-by-side map of lower Manhattan with a building highlighted in yellow, located on Broadway about a block from Wall Street.

"Add in known salvage team activity for today's date and tomorrow," I instructed.

The map on the wall suddenly showed three new highlights in red, green, and blue respectively. There were currently five teams on *Zone Wars*, and one of the government's stipulations regarding the show was complete disclosure of each team's daily location plans. Independent salvage people, like myself, did not have to disclose any information other than designating our chosen Zone entry point and our intended egress site. Proposed trip duration was also collected, but that was just so the Zone border control people could alert our primary contacts if we went overdue. That was it. Nobody would be coming in after us if we didn't come out on our own.

During its four years of production, *Zone War* had followed a total of twelve teams. Seven of them had either died or quit the business during that time. The actual number of salvage people lost in the Zone was easily over a hundred and sixty-two. The survival rate was so low that the production company only occasionally picked new teams and only from people with several years of experience.

Myself, I had close to eight years of experience, most of it with my father. After Brad and JJ Johnson, I was probably the most experienced salvager out there. Flottercot Productions had approached me exactly three times to be on the show, once a year for three years running, but much to the dismay of my sisters, I had turned them down all three times. No way was I allowing a drone camera to follow me around, giving away all my secrets, and there wasn't a camera team anywhere that could survive accompanying me, even if I was to ever give permission. I personally doubted any of them were stupid enough to try. My longevity in the world's deadliest job was directly due to my highly personalized approach and my very customized technology.

"Inform the sender that I agree to attempt the extraction. Strike any guarantee clauses and disclosure amendments," I instructed my AI.

"Done," it replied.

"Okay, now we need to get down to planning."

My father was huge on planning. Massive time was spent on every aspect of a recovery before we ever set foot in the Zone, no detail too small. I could quote every drone's specifications forward and backward by the time I was twelve. Nowadays, two years after his death, I have an exhaustive data bank of information built up in my AI's drives. My planning is still just as thorough, just generally a whole lot faster.

First we reviewed current satellite footage of the building's neighborhood on Broadway, then pulled blueprints on the building itself from the NYC Department of Buildings database. The laptop in question was thought to be on the seventeenth floor, which was gonna be a bitch. Better than the thirty-seventh floor, which the building had, but still, dragging myself, my stealth suit, and my gear up seventeen flights of stairs was gonna suck—hard.

"Suggest carrying cutting torch, bolt cutters, and titanium pry bar. The state of the building is completely unknown. No record of other recoveries occurring at that address."

Great. My AI was right, of course. Getting in and out of multi-story buildings could, and often did, require serious abilities to break and enter. All of my gear was miniaturized, but my pack weight and the resulting suck factor went up with every ounce.

"I'll go through the Brooklyn Battery Tunnel entrance," I decided.

"Concur. That will place you far from the Chelsea Pier entrance. Johnson Recovery and Egorov Salvage are both scheduled for entrance to the Zone at that point tomorrow. Diversion rate is estimated to be sixty-four point eight percent."

Diversion rate was my own proprietary measure, calculated by my AI using satellite footage, *Zone War* production crew drone counts, and my own drone counts measured at the same time if I happened to be in the Zone. I got the idea watching one of the few full episodes I had ever sat through. I had realized that someone or some AI on the studio team kept a running tally of observed drones at the bottom of the screen. The producers used it to raise the viewing tension, as the number would race higher the longer a team was in the Zone and the more noise they made. I, myself, kept a running count of any and all combat units that I observed during my forays, along with the time observed.

After egress, I would give that information along with details on which models and makes I had seen to my AI.

Twenty-five thousand was the estimated number of drones released in the attack, an entire ship's hold's worth. Since that time, thousands had been *killed* or damaged in the course of the passing years and the active action of the salvage crews. The US government paid a hefty bounty for every unit that could be confirmed destroyed, with varying payouts depending on the sophistication and danger each unit posed. Also, Air Force Render drones hunted the high altitudes, preying on any visible drones, and marksman units on barricade duty sniped as many drones as they could see.

There were a couple of mothership drones that had onboard 3D printers that could make small replacement drones, but otherwise the number was estimated to be dwindling, perhaps as low as fifteen thousand drones remaining. Unfortunately, the most lethal and sophisticated units that were the best at killing humans were also best at avoiding their own destruction.

The bounty for an Indian Tiger hunter-killer was north of two hundred thousand dollars, and forget about one of the three remaining Chinese Spider ThreeC units thought to be at large. Each Command, Control, and Communication master drone could orchestrate up to three hundred lesser drones at a time. They had been the most highly advanced units in the Chinese arsenal at the time of the attack, equipped with real, progressive machine-learning software that was capable of rewriting itself to adapt to the battlefield.

One Spider had been destroyed at the end of the second week of the Manhattan attack. That single unit had coordinated battle drones that killed an estimated 230 soldiers, cops, and federal agents. The fact that three such units were still unaccounted for was likely the main reason the military hadn't gone back into Manhattan in force.

So the bounty on a Spider ThreeC was a million dollars. Cheap, if you ask me. You might wonder if we didn't have more advanced drones now, ten years later, that could go in and fight the battles without human lives being lost. We do, and it didn't work. The ThreeCs kept learning, kept adapting, kept growing. They beat the more advanced drones sent against them. In fact, the information in their CPUs, the software that they wrote and rewrote over ten years, would be worth, in my estimation, closer to a billion dollars. Every army on earth would pay up for it.

Some people wonder if any of the ThreeCs are still active, still functioning. I can personally vouch for two. Scariest moment of my life. Eighteen months ago, in the north end of Central Park. I use the Park often, as the drones tend to stay in the more urban areas. Not because they don't function well in the park, but because the park is full of deer and coyotes and a small number of animals that escaped the Central Park Zoo. Combat drones are designed and programmed for killing humans. They ignore animals. But having that many warm bodies clouding their thermal senses is confusing to most drones, costly in processing power. So they tend to stay out of the Park. Which makes the Park one of my favorite places.

Anyway, I was skirting though the woods and came upon the edge of the old softball fields. It was a really nice sunny summer day and I sensed motion out on the overgrown field. Dad's lessons kept me deep in the shadows, peeking over a small hummock of rock and dirt, my low thermal signature camouflage hood over my head. Through my monocular, I saw a veritable army of drones, motionless, solar collectors spread out for maximum charging value. Right in the middle of four tank-killers, seven Tigers, about twenty Russian wolves, and a veritable flock of various flying units were two ThreeCs sitting in the open, charging batteries like the rest. The ThreeCs look like their nickname—spiders—black-painted spiders the size of a sofa loveseat, except these spiders have seven legs, not eight.

The horde stayed that way for an hour, then suddenly the entire battle group of drones activated all at once and flew, crawled, or rolled off to the east, leaving me in a pile of sweat and maybe a little urine. Maybe more than a little.

I bring out dead drones fairly regularly, but mostly just small ones, or I yank the CPUs and ID plates from bigger ones. I don't have a heavy, electro-powered hybrid LAV to haul my catches, so my recorded kills are kinda low. My *actual* kill numbers are a different story. The Zone is my real office and salvage my work—and work is good. Tomorrow I'd head into the Manhattan Drone Zone.

Thanks for reading this introductory snippet of Zone War, the first in the Zone War series, due out late summer, 2018 — John Conroe

I love it, but you're not working on pure Sci-Fi. This has a healthy dystopic element in it. That said, a good dystopia is my absolute catnip, so you'd damn well better pull this off. ☺

Made in the USA
Coppell, TX
14 June 2021